'Come here and I'll sh... again just how perfect y...

He pulled her into his arms, sliding his hands under her T-shirt as he kissed her, leaving her head spinning. He hadn't rejected her. He'd called her perfect. In wonder, she kissed him back while her body melted beneath his touch. Thoughts twirled in her mind until, out of the kaleidoscope of images and words, one truth emerged and flashed behind her closed lids: she was in love with Ned. She was in love with this gorgeous, thoughtful daredevil of a sweet-talking firefighter.

And although she was still scared, although it had been years since a man—or anyone except her sister—had seen her naked, the shock of her realisation was enough to jolt her into action as the pieces of the puzzle fell into place. He hadn't rejected her—and from the way he was talking would it be so very foolish to start hoping this might be more than a one-night stand?

Dear Reader

Life is full of competing wants, needs and desires: having designs on that chocolate versus knowing we've vowed to resist temptation; wanting to stay home on the couch in our slippers when we've already accepted an invitation.

So it's vital that sometimes life makes things easy, with no debate about what we should do. No internal struggle. No guilt. Just pleasure.

It's in whole-hearted support of this Pleasure Principle that I give you Ned Kellaway, the charismatic firefighting hero of THE PLAYBOY FIREFIGHTER'S PROPOSAL.

If you've read my last book, EMERGENCY: WIFE NEEDED, you've already made Ned's acquaintance. Ned is a shameless playboy with a life-is-for-the-living attitude, and—I admit it—I was his from the first. I just had to spend more time with him.

Ned was born with a thirst for all things action. He's the team leader for the Fire Service's Emergency Response team. Built to make any girl feel protected, he's also scorching in the looks department. And, although no woman has been able to get inside his head, none are complaining about getting inside his bed. It's going to take a pretty special woman to make him question his playboy lifestyle and get him to face his own past. Is Sarah Richardson, emergency consultant, the woman to do it?

So grab some chocolate, find somewhere cosy, turn the page and meet Ned Kellaway. And when you're interrupted, as you surely will be, ignore all demands and put your nose back in the book! Trust me, the right to indulge in a book is definitely enshrined as a Pleasure Principle.

Love

Emily Forbes

THE PLAYBOY FIREFIGHTER'S PROPOSAL

BY
EMILY FORBES

MILLS & BOON™

Pure reading pleasure™

First published in Great Britain 2009
Harlequin Mills & Boon Limited,
Eton House, 18-24 Paradise Road, Richmond, Surrey TW9 1SR

© Emily Forbes 2009

ISBN: 978 0 263 86840 1

Set in Times Roman 10½ on 12¾ pt
03-0409-48609

Printed and bound in Spain
by Litografia Rosés, S.A., Barcelona

Emily Forbes is the pseudonym of two sisters who share both a passion for writing and a life-long love of reading. Beyond books and their families, their interests include cooking (food is a recurring theme in their books!), learning languages, playing the piano and netball, as well as an addiction to travel—armchair is fine, but anything involving a plane ticket is better. Home for both is South Australia, where they live three minutes apart with their husbands and four young children. With backgrounds in business administration, law, arts, clinical psychology and physiotherapy, they have worked in many areas. This past professional experience adds to their writing in many ways: legal dilemmas, psychological ordeals and business scandals are all intermeshed with the medical settings of their stories. And, since nothing could ever be as delicious as spending their days telling the stories of gorgeous heroes and spirited heroines, they are eternally grateful their mutual dream of writing for a living came true.

They would love you to visit and keep up to date with current news and future releases at the Medical™ Romance authors' website: http://www.medicalromance.com/

Recent titles by the same author:

WEDDING AT PELICAN BEACH
THE SURGEON'S LONGED-FOR BRIDE
A MOTHER IN THE MAKING
EMERGENCY AT PELICAN BEACH

My darling littlest daughter, you came into our lives just as this book was being finished, so it's only right this one is for you. We waited a long time for you, and the moment we saw you it all made sense: we were meant to be together. You have enriched our world in so many ways already, daily bringing us joy and sunshine and laughter. May the future shower you with every blessing and may you always know how very dear you are to all of us and how greatly you are loved.

From my heart to yours and back again,

Your loving Mummy

CHAPTER ONE

NED KELLAWAY scanned the racecourse from his vantage point in the grandstand, absorbing the impact as the disarray grew before his eyes. It was chaos, utter chaos, and far worse than he'd anticipated.

He was loving every minute of it.

He'd love it even more if he could get down there into the thick of things. Instead, when the emergency services and medical response teams arrived on site, he'd have to sit back and watch as they responded to the crisis. 'Sit back and watch' were not words in his vocabulary.

His gaze swept the area again as he marvelled at how all his planning had successfully brought this to fruition. Littering the ground in front of him were dozens and dozens of prostrate bodies, some immobile, many struggling to their feet, most bloodied. Voices carried up to him on the breeze as people called out in pain. Just as many were lying silently.

The adrenalin coursing through his body made it an almost impossible feat to simply stand and observe. The mass casualties would require medical attention and there were fatalities, too, requiring a response of a different sort. He mentally checked off the list of things that needed to happen, including the task of overseeing the rollout of all the emergency response teams, a role that would normally be his since his skills in this area were second to none. Today, his expertise was exactly the reason why he wasn't down there, taking control. He was needed for another task. But that didn't mean he was finding it easy, sitting here, excluded from the action, prevented from taking control and restoring order, watching someone else do his job.

In the midst of the chaos was a fifty-seater bus, now containing considerably fewer than fifty seats, and this drew his focus. The bus's left-hand side had been ripped open by the force of the explosion, the metal casing peeled back like a tin can, its interior exposed. Above the back wheels, where there should have been a row of seats, was a gaping hole. Luggage was strewn on the ground around the bus and lying amongst the bags were the injured passengers.

In the time Ned had taken to process the scene a few passengers had gathered their wits and were now moving between the prone figures. It wasn't clear if they were trying to offer assistance, staggering about in shock or simply searching for people lost in the confusion.

To his right, a second bomb had detonated inside the bus terminal and more people were pouring out of the building, further congesting the space around the damaged bus. Visibility was compromised by smoke, a fact that would create another set of problems for the emergency teams.

The noise was increasing now as people realised what had happened. Voices rang out, yelling over the top of one another in an effort to be heard, growing louder and more desperate as the seconds ticked on.

Ned took a deep breath, anticipation of the imminent arrival of the emergency service vehicles sending more adrenalin through his system. He rubbed his hands over his head, leaving his short hair sticking up at all angles, as he cast his gaze across the scene once more.

And then he heard sirens. The bomb victims heard them too and ceased their yelling momentarily as they listened to confirm the sound.

The emergency personnel were on their way.

The first crews to arrive would be from the fire department. He glanced at the stopwatch in his hand, timing the response. Getting here quickly was the easy part—the real tests were all in front of the men and women hurtling towards the racecourse, with scant knowledge as to what they'd be facing on arrival.

But from where he was standing, having to watch was a hundred times harder than dealing with disaster hands on.

Sarah stood a couple of rows behind the others. She needed the extra height and it was the only way to get it since stiletto heels weren't an option in her line of work. If ever she was keen for a view, it was today, to watch the planned event unfold. With her clipboard in one hand and a pen in the other, she stood rocking on her heels on the top step, clicking the pen on and off as she watched the scene below. Most of the bomb victims were milling around in a dazed manner. It wasn't easy for her as a trained emergency doctor to sit back and observe but today that's what her job was. As part of the team who'd put this training exercise together, it was her role to instruct the medical members of the first responder unit, those men and women who were the first emergency personnel on the scene at any disasters classed as CBR—chemical, biological or radiological—incidents.

And there was no use pretending she wasn't just as aware of Ned Kellaway. It didn't escape her notice that he, like her, had tilted his head a touch to the side as the sirens became audible. It didn't escape her notice that he was as focused, professional and in control as she'd have expected from the man she'd come to know a little over these last weeks as they'd worked together to bring today to fruition. And it didn't escape her notice that, despite all this, he was as breathtakingly charismatic as ever. If anything, these surroundings only added to his many attractions. It must be the whole men-in-uniform thing, she told herself, so as not to be too badly distracted from the training simulation.

It was what they were here for, after all. The moment of truth. After weeks of planning, they were about to see how the teams performed. The sense of excitement was mixed with tense anxiety in case any of them fell below standard, a guaranteed result of the day. Which team would prove to be the weakest link? Glancing along the rows below her at the people she'd worked with intensively she saw Lucas, from the police force, and Neill, from the State Emergency Services, were deep in discussion. Angie, the liaison officer for the ambulance service, was standing slightly apart, seemingly focused on scanning the arena below. They all had to be taut with expectation but she could see no outward signs. Hopefully her own tumult of feelings was similarly veiled.

A few policemen were already on site but larger numbers of police and paramedics would follow the fire department. If the disaster was on a large enough scale doctors would be called to the scene from the city hospitals' emergency departments. That would happen here. Soon.

Today's disaster was large-scale. It had been planned that way.

The fire department would be responsible for controlling the situation and her team would be under their command.

Thinking of the fire department inevitably bought her attention back to the man who, in a real-life situation, would most likely be the incident controller.

Ned Kellaway. A station officer with the Metropolitan Fire Service, he was currently the man in charge of the first responder unit, which included all the emergency service departments as well as the medicos.

Since he was sitting below her, a few seats to her right, she could observe him without him knowing. Of all the members of the team, he'd made the biggest impression on her. And on every other female whose path he'd crossed. The man had universal appeal. She'd seen his charm in action as he'd bantered with the females on the team, herself included. And there was no denying she'd found herself enjoying it when it had been directed her way.

Now he was sitting on the edge of his chair, leaning forwards as though the seat was too small to contain his big frame. His elbows propped on his knees and his chin resting on his hands, he appeared to be concentrating hard.

His fireman's casual uniform, a short-sleeved navy T-shirt, stencilled with 'MFS' across the back, showed off tanned, muscular arms and hugged his torso. His broad shoulders were nicely square and his back tapered to a narrow waist. She knew he worked out as there wasn't an ounce of excess weight on him. His short brown hair was spiking up. He had a habit of running his fingers through it, leaving it standing on end. Did he know he did that?

Then again, more importantly, why did *she* know it was a habit? Had she really been paying him that much attention? She scanned his rear view again, noting the turbulence in her belly that had little to do with the drama unfolding below them and everything to do with finding Ned ridiculously attractive. No use denying it, she'd mastered paying him attention.

The sirens were at earsplitting levels now, indicating the pace below was about to pick up. Ned made a move to stand and she ran hungry eyes over the stretch of his T-shirt across his back as he eased himself from his chair. He turned to the group at large and suggested they all join him so they could discuss the event as it progressed.

The day was about to spin to a whole new level and there'd be no more opportunities for meaningless fantasies. She may be new to this side of emergency medicine, her CBR training may only be recent and largely untested, but she'd worked for several years in the emergency department of Adelaide's biggest hospital and she knew when craziness was about to happen.

She'd save her mental images of the man in the dark blue T-shirt for later.

There was no risk of her fantasies coming to anything, but that didn't mean she couldn't indulge in a harmless bit of daydreaming later on. When the team was disbanded and she and Ned Kellaway no longer crossed paths, she'd be glad of the daydream material. She shelved her vague feeling of unease that she'd be diving into her store of memories the first chance she got. Tonight, maybe.

Sarah Richardson was in control.

Sarah Richardson was not looking for a relationship. Or casual sex. Or anything that involved taking her clothes off, for that matter.

Which, she told herself as she followed the others down the stairs to gather in the aisle with Ned, was exactly why it was about time she had a store of knee-weakening, butterfly-inducing images to keep her company.

Men were not an option.

The group came together, forming a cluster along the balcony railing, awaiting the imminent swarm of emergency crews.

Of all the group, only one held Ned's personal interest.

Sarah.

He watched her as she made her way to where he stood. She had a determined expression in her grey eyes, eyes that gave her petite features a gravity and depth that was intriguing. He was finding out that he liked intriguing. Very much.

In the numerous hours this team had spent together over the last weeks, he'd got a handle on most of the group, with the notable exception of Dr Sarah Richardson, who was still proving a bit of a mystery. She commanded respect and had been on top of her game in the hours of meetings, despite the fact she was relatively new to CBR work. On those few occasions when they'd gone for a drink at the end of the day or taken a coffee-break, he'd liked her tendency to sit back and observe, then add a droll remark that neatly summed up the matter under discussion or had him in stitches. Hers was an intellect quietly on show but not paraded to make others feel inferior.

Considerate, respectful of others' views. There were plenty of words he'd come up with to describe her. And yet he was still grappling with a very real sense of knowing nothing about her, a sense she was holding back something of herself. She was definitely more reserved than the rest, and several times he'd sensed she'd started to let her guard down but the next time they'd met the barriers would be up again. She seemed almost wary of him. Who knew why that was? But he had a feeling that if he could discover her secret it would be worth the effort.

Sarah came quietly to his side, the group now complete. What would she do if she knew he was interested? Most women made their attraction to him quite obvious, yet Sarah seemed immune to him. The thrill of the unknown coursed through him. Combined with the challenges of today, the feeling of being on the brink of uncharted territory was heady stuff.

Suppressing a secret half-grin, he crouched to pick up the whiteboard at his feet, straightening as the leading fire appliance pulled up and the firefighters emerged from the cabin, wearing full protective gear, ready to deal with this emergency. His team. The knowledge sent yet another rush of excitement flooding through his veins.

He glanced at the whiteboard on which he'd written the duties and responsibilities of the first responders so each task could be checked off and comments added as the observing team thought of them.

The police and paramedics arrived hot on the heels of the fire department. Ned turned to Lucas and Angie, the police and ambulance liaison officers, who were standing on his right, and angled his whiteboard so everyone could see the list as he read out the next item and they each concentrated on checking off their team's roles. Conversation had stopped when the fire crews had appeared, their white-suited bulk intimidating even to this group of experts.

'Isolate the incident and secure perimeter,' said Ned, quoting from the whiteboard the procedure he knew by heart.

'Easier said than done,' Lucas commented. 'Now I can actually see it, it's almost impossible for my people to secure the area.' The injured commuters were actors, hired for the day to play specific roles—walking wounded, unconscious, seriously injured, unharmed and dead—and they were all giving award-winning performances.

'Securing the area was always going to be a challenge,' Ned replied. 'An open arena like this is the hardest to contain. That's what makes it the perfect test scenario. And as for the actors, it's probably a career highlight for most of them. No surprise they're playing it to the hilt but they seem to be following directions.'

'I imagine that's proving hard,' said Sarah, and Ned

found himself giving her his full attention, much more so than to Lucas, 'for those actors told to be mortally wounded and lie still. Can you imagine lying motionless while everyone around you is getting their big break, running amok, covered in fake blood and screaming?'

Ned laughed. 'You think we might have real need for the medicos when the bad blood spills? Hope you're ready for action.' She had no idea how much he hoped she was ready for some action.

He turned his attention back to the racecourse, adjusting his earpiece to listen in on the fire department's frequency. Each of the exercise-writing team observing had an earpiece to listen to their own team's conversations without interfering with each other. The others in the group peeled off nearby to discuss and watch, leaving Ned pleased with how things had worked out: he had Sarah to himself, for the next little while at least.

'Ned, I've never seen a simulation like this and I'll never get to see this stage if there's a real situation,' Sarah said. 'Medicos wouldn't be on the scene yet. Can you explain what everyone's doing, if it won't interrupt your assessment?'

Things were getting better and better. Now she was seeking out his time, thinking it might be an inconvenience when it was nothing but a pleasure.

'Sure. And as for finding it hard to make sense of it down there, remember none of us has organised something on this scale before. This is a first for Adelaide and it's a lot easier to follow on paper. I was part of simulations in my CBR training in Canada last year but never from this angle. I was in the thick of the action. Today is just as much about giving this team…' he indicated their group '…training in overall management as it is about getting the specialists down there ready…' he nodded at the racecourse '…if there's ever such an event.' Ned located his IC as he spoke. 'You see Tony down there?' He pointed to where a man was standing about ten feet east of the bus. 'He's the acting incident controller. He's doing my job today. First, he's trying to establish control, making sure everyone is doing what he's asked them to or knows their role. He's got to know what's going on at all times. He'll get the "warm zone" set up around him, sealing off the bus and the terminal. You'd deal with him once you arrived at the scene, as you know.'

She nodded, totally absorbed in the scene below them and his descriptions. If he moved just a few inches to his right, they'd be touching. The thought was delicious.

'Triage happens inside the "warm zone" before victims are moved through into the "cold zone" for treatment, evacuation or assembly,' she quoted from the procedure they knew so well, presumably oblivious to the effect she was having on him. 'How do you think the police are managing with making sure people don't leave the scene?'

'I won't trespass on Lucas's turf by commenting, but I can tell you the bomb squad is getting warm on their search for other explosive devices.' He touched her arm to show her where he was looking.

'So there are more out there.' She flicked him a sideways glance, curiosity sparkling in her eyes. 'Not just the two we've already seen?'

'Let's see what they find.' Ned grinned. 'The whole point of this exercise is to test everyone's skills—may as well go the whole hog.'

She laughed. 'Somehow I think going for broke comes naturally to you,' she said before turning away again quickly, like she'd said too much and unintentionally strayed into personal territory. 'And the firemen going into the betting ring, what are they doing?' Her change of topic was swift but he stored the information away with relish: he had to have been on her mind for her to make a personal comment about him.

'They'll be taking readings to check for any radioactive signals. They'll also check for flammable gases and check oxygen levels. The site is pretty open so that shouldn't be a problem but we don't want people leaving the scene if there's been any contamination.'

Sarah held her hand up to her ear as information came through her earpiece. 'The call's gone out for more medical support. Let's see how long it takes the hospital team to get here.'

'How long do you reckon?'

'Fifteen minutes from either the city or down south.'

'Though they're expecting this callout, so in a real event you'd have to add on an extra ten minutes to give them time to get ready to go.'

'So the paramedics will do their thing for about half an hour before we'd even get here?'

'That's it, but in a situation like this there'll still be plenty of work for your team.'

People were starting to gather at the assembly point now. Victims who were mobile were being directed to the police officers who would take statements in case anyone had any pertinent information. They would also keep a list of names to help with enquiries. Those people who were hurt but didn't need treatment on site would be transported to the nearest hospitals but only once it had been determined if there was any contamination. It was imperative the site be contained until that was confirmed or ruled out. Ned noticed a line of ambulances coming onto the racecourse, arriving in an almost constant stream now, closely followed by the media.

'Take a look at that,' Ned said to Sarah as he jotted times and notes on his whiteboard. 'The newshounds arrived before your guys.'

'How did they know to come?'

'They monitor 000 calls.'

'But there haven't been any emergency calls. This is a training exercise.'

'I might have had something to do with that. Call it a dose of reality for the crews down there. Having to deal with television cameras trying to get the perfect shot for the evening news will test most of us. Tony will have to release a statement and the reporters will be after interviews with the section chiefs.'

'You've thought of everything.' He was pretty sure that was appreciation in her voice.

'We'll soon find out.'

'What happens now?'

'My guys will let your lot through to areas that have been declared safe and the paramedics will direct you to the most critically injured. Basically, triage continues with more hands on deck. Now all the teams have arrived, it's time we went down into the thick of things.

It's far easier to find out what problems they're experiencing while it's happening, rather than waiting for feedback later.'

Without waiting for an answer he reached over the seat in front of him and grabbed a handful of fluorescent jackets marked 'Fire Department'. 'We'd better put these on inside out. We don't want to be given jobs to do,' he said with a grin. 'We just want to blend into the crowd.' He shrugged into the orange jacket and picked up his two-way radio.

Together, they ducked and weaved through the crowds. In the thick of the chaos it was difficult to get a good grasp of the scenario, and difficult to sort the high noise levels into anything meaningful. The wail of sirens split the air periodically as emergency vehicles continued to arrive. Closer to the centre of the scene, the moans of the injured competed with the shouted instructions and directions from the emergency teams, who were trying to restore some semblance of order.

The noises, particularly those of the victims, were manufactured but it gave an accurate sense of how difficult it would be in a real scenario to determine who needed priority attention. Everywhere, injured people lay, sat and stumbled, making progress through the throng slow.

'How hard is it to be among all these potential patients and not be able to roll up your sleeves?'

She thought for a moment. 'Disconcerting. But that might be more to do with the fact that the more enthusiastic actors among them are coming up with sounds I've never heard in any emergency department. We've covered all bases on making this seem realistic,' she added. 'Adelaide will be fresh out of fake blood and sheets after today.' She indicated the sheets covering the 'deceased' around them. 'It's hard to remember this is a set-up.' She nodded discreetly towards an elderly gentleman walking by them, a dazed expression on his face and blood running down the side of his head from a gash over his temple.

A few paces further on Ned stopped, his hand to his ear again. 'My guys have found something suspicious inside the terminal. I'm going to go and see how they deal with it. I'll catch up with you at tomorrow's review session, if not later today.'

He left her on that note, putting it out there that he wanted to see her again but giving nothing away. He might have said the same thing to a mate. Instinctively, he knew not to rush this one. If mysteries lurked behind those grey eyes, as he suspected, rushing her was not the way to play this. The one sure thing he wanted was to give himself his best chance at uncovering Sarah's secrets.

He loved a challenge.

Max, one of his best mates, had once said all it took for Ned to show an interest in someone was for them to possess two X chromosomes. He liked to think he was a little more discerning, although Max had been closer to the truth than was comfortable.

Applying Max's theory to Sarah, there was no denying she possessed many of the attributes that attracted Ned—a sense of humour, long hair and definitely the right chromosomes. Basically she was a woman and that made her attractive to Ned. But she was different from the women who normally caught his eye, the type who were usually after a good time and nothing more. Ned didn't do 'something more'.

So it was all the more intriguing to wonder why Sarah had caught his eye. She was brunette, not blonde. She was slim where his usual type was curvy. She was too slim to be called sexy. Sensual? He intended to find out.

He reached the betting ring, which had been set up as the pseudo–bus terminal. Time to put Sarah out of his mind. It was essential as he had precious little room to indulge in fantasies today.

Besides, the degree to which she intrigued him could only be about the challenge. It was all about the chase.

And there was plenty of time for that tomorrow.

CHAPTER TWO

HER urge to fidget was nearing the point of compulsion. Being cooped up in the meeting room at police headquarters to review the simulated exercise of the preceding day was wearing thin. Luckily, Ned was there to provide some distraction.

She figured they had at least another hour to go before they'd be finished and right now the matter under discussion didn't involve her. It was between the police and ambulance teams and Lucas and Angie had it covered so she was free to steal glances at Ned.

He'd been very much on her mind since yesterday. Images of a seriously attractive fireman with mischievous green eyes, a cheeky grin and a physique that was hard in all the right places and shaped just as nature intended had kept popping into her head. So much so she found it a bit unsettling now he was back in front of her again. It was impossible to ignore him.

He was lounging in his chair and even that posture seemed to work in his favour. He looked easy in his skin. And easy on the eyes. His dark blue uniform was spotless, the trousers were pressed, T-shirt tucked in and fitted to his body, leaving no unsightly creases. As usual, he'd been running his fingers through his hair, leaving it sticking up in tufts. The dishevelled look enhanced his larrikin air.

Was it any wonder she was finding it hard to focus?

Sighing over a man wouldn't keep her where she needed to be, which was in the safe place she'd made for herself since she'd got Alistair out of her life, or rather since Alistair had ditched her unceremoniously. She'd perfected the art of self-protection when it came to men—why sigh with longing over a guy who was a threat to that security? She should be troubled to find she had diminishing control over her thoughts when it came to Ned. Losing control meant being vulnerable.

Vulnerable was a state she'd sworn never to be in again.

Alistair. The name swam into mind, her old mantra, the one that never failed to remind her why self-protection was essential and messing about with men was for fools.

Yet there was something about Ned that was making it increasingly difficult to remember any of those hard-learned lessons.

That was four times now he'd sprung her stealing glances at him. By the time the team review had finished he was almost bursting to get to her side and make the most of her apparent interest. There wouldn't be many more meetings like this and when they were finished he'd have to be more obvious about wanting to spend time with her. Maximising his opportunities was the way to go.

'You might have the others fooled, but I know where your mind was just now,' he said in a quiet voice, for her alone. 'You can't look that serene if you're thinking about work.'

Maybe she hadn't been thinking about him. Maybe she'd been daydreaming and oblivious to the fact she'd simply been staring at him, but, judging by the faint bloom of pink dusting her cheeks at his comment, perhaps it wasn't a vain hope. Perhaps she wasn't as immune to him as she'd seemed.

She didn't answer straight away, continuing to gather her papers, a slight smile on her lips, her perfect white teeth worrying at her full bottom lip as she snapped each rubber band and attached each bulldog clip exactly so on each bundle of papers with long fingers before sliding each highlighter pen neatly into its plastic case.

He'd never been the slightest bit interested in unravelling the mysteries of women's apparently universal love affair with stationery. But now? Watching Sarah sort her pens in an obvious order, not just one after the other, but some at this end of that packet, another there, it occurred to him that if there was a woman in the world who could make stationery fascinating, he was looking at her.

'If I was looking serene…' Her tone was light and cheery without any trace of the embarrassment or confusion he'd glimpsed initially. 'Then I must have been thinking about the shoe sale I'm ducking out to at lunch.'

'Not buying it,' he said good-naturedly. 'But I am buying coffee. And since we all planned on being here for at least another hour, you can't say you're needed back at work.'

Sarah had finished gathering her things and he held the door open for her as they walked to the lifts.

'I wasn't going to,' she said as she glanced up at him before entering the lift. 'But at last count I've had three cups of coffee this morning.'

Bending his head close to hers, he said softly, 'You're not answering my question.'

'I'm not?'

'Telling me how much caffeine you've had doesn't tell me whether you want more. With me.'

'Ah.' She smiled as the lift doors opened at the ground floor and his spirits rose anew. She glanced at a giant metal clock suspended on the rear wall of the foyer and apparently discerned the time from the bare face and the single razor-sharp hand before he'd even been sure it was a clock. 'I have half an hour but, really, if I have any more coffee I'll be flying back to work. As it is, I'd better walk back to get rid of some of these caffeine jitters.'

She was definitely looking agitated but the pink in her cheeks and the way she wasn't quite meeting his eyes suggested any jitters weren't from the caffeine. Did he make her nervous or was she as aware of the energy between them as he was?

'You have to walk past the fire station. I'll walk with you.'

'You don't want a coffee?'

'I'm trying to cut down,' he said, laughing, letting her know that wasn't the slightest bit true, and the coffee had only been a reason to be with her. Walking would do just as well.

They turned right onto the street and headed up through the city. He automatically shortened his long strides so she could keep pace as he chatted to her about her work and answered her questions about the simulated exercise.

And all the while, he was working towards one thing: eroding whatever notion she'd got into her very appealing mind that she should keep her distance. Sure, she'd come along every time he'd suggested coffee or a drink but only once she'd been sure the others were going to be there, too. Why was that? He wanted her; he was confident now the interest was mutual. So why the hesitation to explore it?

There was a lot more to Sarah Richardson than looks and brains. If he didn't figure out why he couldn't get her out of his head, he was going to go crazy.

'What does the rest of the day hold for you?' Sarah asked as they came into sight of the station.

'More paperwork for the CBR training and when that's done I practise looking busy.'

'How do you do that exactly?' Sarah looked at him, a gleam of amusement in her eyes. Her question gave him the flash of inspiration he was waiting for. Genius!

'Come in and I'll show you. There's a knack to it.'

They'd reached the station and were standing before the massive glass doors that were tall enough to allow the biggest of the engines to exit and enter. A row of shiny red fire engines was visible through the glass. 'Can I?'

He did a mental punch of the air. He should have invited her for a private tour of the station weeks ago.

'You can and you shall.' He placed a hand on the small of her back, relishing the body warmth coming through her shirt, telling himself the desire kicking up and down his spine wasn't anything out of the ordinary.

It was all about the challenge.

Why, then, was he filled with a sudden urge to show

her how good he was at his job and a rush of excitement that he was about to get the opportunity?

The equation was simple: if she wanted him and he wanted her, chemistry would take care of all the little details. He could sit back and enjoy letting the attraction unfold.

The niggling sense of pressure to make a good impression didn't mean anything.

It was craziness, pure and simple, but she could have clapped her hands with glee when he'd asked her to see the station. She resisted giving such a physical demonstration of her pleasure. Just. She didn't manage to disguise it completely, though. The cool, calm and collected woman she'd intended to present herself as wouldn't have said quite so excitedly, 'What can I see first?'

'Enthusiastic tour groups, that's the sort we like.' He led her through one of the open doors, between two huge fire engines, until they were standing in the central area of the station, looking past the vehicles out to the city street.

'The fire trucks are all different,' she said, waving a hand along the row of vehicles while mentally giving her fears about men a swift kick into submission. It was just a visit to the fire station, something she'd be keen to do with or without Ned playing tour guide, she tried to convince herself.

'Appliances,' Ned said.

She must have looked confused. For a moment she had almost looked around for a white-goods section.

'They're called appliances, not trucks.'

She thought about it for a moment and then nodded.

'You're not going to make a crack about us driving around in toasters and washing machines?'

'The thought never crossed my mind,' she lied, as she smiled innocently at him.

'In that case, it's settled. You get the extra-special tour reserved for extra-special people who don't make cracks about firemen. The burden we bear for the good of the city,' he added on a dramatic note.

'A thespian in a fireman's pants?'

'You'd be surprised what you'd find inside a fireman's pants.' The sparkle in his eyes told her he was fully aware of the innuendo in his comment.

Who could blame her if her cheeks flamed to match the appliances?

'Get your mind out of the gutter,' he teased. 'I'm speaking figuratively.'

'Like I should know that. But you can't stop now. Titillate me with tales of firemen's pants.'

'There you go again,' he said, shaking his head at her as they walked to the largest of the engines and he leant against it with a casual air, perfectly in his element and posing more danger by the minute to her already wobbly equilibrium. 'But since you really want to know, I'll let you inside just a few of the pairs of pants around this joint. We have an artist, a nurse...' he held up a hand and counted them off on his fingers '...a carpenter, several professional footballers...' He started the count again with his right hand. 'A builder and a chef.'

'So I shouldn't be surprised at what I find? Even a thespian?'

'Sure, why not?' He straightened up and pulled open

the door of the vehicle as if it was made of paper, not the huge, heavy thing she knew it was. 'And if I ever come across one, I'll be sure to introduce you.'

He sent her a wink that turned her insides to jelly and then motioned her over. She floated across as if under a spell. That was some wink. And now, between his bulk, all broad shoulders and long, lean height, and the huge vehicle rising up beside them, she felt delightfully feminine.

Was this why firefighters were so attractive? They made women feel small and delicate and safe? Even a woman who prided herself on never needing to rely on a man for protection? She shrugged off the thought as being the crazy bit of fluff it was. Since when had feeling like a guy could, and would if the need arose, protect her become a turn-on?

'Climb aboard. Your magical mystery tour is about to begin.' Once again he placed his hand on the small of her back as she started to climb up into the cab. The feel of his large hand through the cotton of her shirt was delicious and far too distracting. So much so she could mentally outline exactly where the tip of each finger was resting.

But the familiar anxiety was there, too, that always came with a man's touch. The anxiety wasn't as powerful as she would have expected, though, not as powerful as the attraction she was feeling. Normally her anxiety would increase proportionately, but strangely it wasn't happening. Yes, the niggle of self-consciousness was there, but here she was, experiencing an attraction more intense than she could ever remember feeling, and she wasn't feeling totally overwhelmed.

On the contrary, he was so close his scent was filling

her head and making it spin in a way that left no doubt she was drawn to him. Each time she took a breath, the rush of desire was strong and coursed through her body. He smelt of woods and the outdoors, the blend heady and original. She just knew it hadn't come out of a bottle, or, if it had, it had mixed with his own natural scent so that it was now his own. If a company could package it, they'd be on to a sure hit. Women would buy it simply to put on their pillows and go to sleep dreaming of a man like Ned.

She lost the smell of him when he closed the cab door behind her, but in seconds he had come around the other side of the truck—oops, the appliance—and was springing into the driver's seat beside her. She edged closer to take another breath. If scent could be addictive, she was already there and it was a struggle to get her mouth to work and form any words to break the silence.

'You didn't tell me which one of those descriptions fits you.' When he looked at her, she added, 'Are you the poet? The footballer? The chef?'

'None of the above,' he said as he flicked switches and brought the appliance to life, buttons and lights flashing on the console and across a bewildering array of levers and headsets and gadgets. 'Since I've taken on the role of training co-ordinator for the first response unit I'm one of the few without a second job beyond the service. I'm very much full-time here now.'

'And before?'

He laughed. 'I was addicted to extreme sports. Still am, in fact, just don't get quite the same time for it now.'

'Extreme sports?' She looked at him to check if he

was serious. He didn't look like he was joking. He was still reading dials, not waiting for her reaction. 'Like free-climbing and base-jumping?'

'Very much like that.'

The emergency doctor in her was horrified. The woman in her was undeniably impressed. Impressed and begging for more images to add to her fantasy bank.

'I thought base-jumping was illegal in Australia?'

'In some states it is but I haven't done that yet. But if it's legal and not just downright stupid, I'll give it a go.'

'Were you born an adrenalin junkie?'

He laughed and the sound wrapped around her like a familiar blanket. His dimple flashed in his cheek and his green eyes sparkled. He had one of the most contagious laughs she'd ever heard, a laugh that said life was fun and full of interesting things.

'I started off slow—Mum took me to swimming lessons when I was six and I absolutely loved the water. That led to triathlons and once I'd done the Hawaiian Ironman the next challenge was extreme sports.'

'The Hawaiian Ironman—that's the one with a ten-kilometre swim and finishes with a marathon?'

'It's only a three-and-a-bit-kilometre swim.' He grinned at her. 'But don't forget the one-hundred-and-eighty-k bike ride.'

'And you completed it?'

'Yep. A long way behind the leaders, I must admit.'

'That's still pretty amazing. No wonder you need to jump off buildings now.'

'Well, I haven't actually done that yet. Perhaps you should come with me some time?'

'Sure.' He turned to her, his expression a mix of

pleasure and surprise, probably more like astonishment. Yep, she was pretty sure it would be astonishment as she was gob-smacked at her reply, too.

'What exactly did you just agree to?'

She did a quick mental back-flip and came up with a save. 'To watching you do something crazy.'

He tipped his head back and laughed again. 'Touché.'

'Isn't it more fun being a hero with an audience?'

'Hero? My mum would argue that point with you.' He sent her a sidelong grin that had her gripping the seat cover with her fingernails. 'But I never say no to an appreciative audience.'

'I don't think it's in a mum's job description to encourage risk-taking.' The words came out in a burbled rush. She was still reeling from that grin. 'What does your dad think? Or did you get your daredevil side from him?'

'My dad died when I was little, but I think he was similarly inclined, at least before he had children. He was a fireman too—I think lots of us have that need for an adrenalin rush.'

His voice hadn't changed when he'd answered her, he'd taken her question in his stride and his tone had dismissed the possibility of giving him any sympathy. He'd had an enormous loss as a little boy but it was quite clear he didn't want her sympathy. She knew how that felt, so she wasn't sure there was anything to read into it. They hardly knew each other, and she wasn't rushing to confide her own losses and fears to him. For now, she'd leave it at that.

She followed his descriptions and asked myriad questions as he showed her through one appliance before explaining the other, different types. The station would have been intriguing no matter who was showing her around, but as it was Ned, it was that much better. He kept his commentary up with behind-the-scenes stories until she was enjoying herself so immensely she forgot about the anxiety pooled low in her belly.

He showed her through the whole station, including the gym, kitchen and sleeping quarters, before they ended the tour back where they had started over an hour before. He took that as a good sign. He hadn't seen her look at her watch once, and she'd said she only had thirty minutes. This was not a woman keen to get away and if he knew anything, he'd swear she'd enjoyed herself with him. She'd relaxed and her laughter had come easily as he'd regaled her with his funniest stories of station life.

When had he last enjoyed a woman's company so much, beyond the bedroom or in it? If it was about the chase, the signs were pointing towards a good outcome. But the signal that it was something more was still emitting a low-grade bleep somewhere in the back of his mind. Sarah was nothing like the usual women who sauntered up to him at the pub. Maybe that's all it was.

'Now, it doesn't seem right that you know all there is to know about me but I still don't know the first thing about what you do in your spare time.'

'What I do? Spare time?' She said the words like they were foreign to her.

Perhaps they were.

He gave her a little push in the direction he was really after. Subtlety wasn't his middle name. According to his fellow firies, that honour went to charm. 'Downtime for Sarah. You go out to dinner with your boyfriend. You paint. You go for long, romantic walks on the beach at sunset with your boyfriend. You enjoy cooking. You prefer spending cosy evenings at home on the couch, watching old black and white movies…'

'With my boyfriend,' she volunteered.

'So you have a boyfriend?' His voice sounded normal but he didn't think he'd been quick enough to disguise his reaction to her words.

'No, I don't, but you seemed so keen on the idea I didn't want to disappoint you.' She was laughing openly at him, enjoying herself at his expense, and he didn't mind a bit. Not now he knew he was free to pursue her as much as his heart desired.

'You haven't.' He left her to figure that one out and charged ahead. 'Back to the point—spare time and you don't go together. You're not knocking me over with your list of extra-curricular activities. I can't know where to take you on our first date if I don't know what you like.'

'You want to take me out? On a date?'

For a moment he thought he'd jumped the gun. Perhaps she wasn't as interested as he was. He wasn't used to women hesitating but then she smiled. That didn't help.

'Are you smiling a "Yes, I'll go out with you" or "I'm going to really enjoy turning him down" sort of smile?'

'Neither.' She met his eyes now. 'But it's a yes.'

The lines of concentration running across his forehead disappeared as his green eyes crinkled upwards with the smile—no, grin—that spread across his face. What a way to make a girl feel special. Ned had that talent down pat. She hadn't intended to accept a date but he was hard to resist.

'What about this weekend?' They'd walked back to the door they'd first entered through, and he was leaning nonchalantly against the doorframe, his hands shoved deep in his pockets.

'No good. I'm shopping for wedding shoes with my sister.'

'More shoes! You can't possibly shop all weekend for shoes and I hope it's for her wedding and not yours as you just told me you don't have a boyfriend.'

'Shoe-shopping is only part of the weekend and, yes, it is my sister's wedding. Saturday night I'm going to a charity dinner.'

'A hospital fundraiser?'

'No, it's the dinner to kick off National Organ Donor Awareness Week. I'm often a guest speaker for them.'

'Intriguing. And admirable.'

For a brief moment Sarah wondered about asking Ned to accompany her. She was always offered the option of bringing a guest, but she'd never taken a proper date. How would it feel to walk in on Ned's arm dressed in her evening dress and him in black tie? For once she wouldn't feel like the only partnerless person in the room, the one everyone wondered about.

How would it feel to walk in with him and know that every woman there, young or old, single or taken, would be sneaking glances, wishing she could trade places with her?

The undisguised interest in his eyes was clear. 'You seem to have a fascinatingly rich internal life.'

'I'm sorry.'

'Don't be. By the expressions skittering across your face, it was a more interesting conversation than many I've actually been part of. I enjoyed putting thoughts to your expressions.'

'What did you come up with?'

'That you were debating whether to invite me to your dinner on Saturday night.'

She nearly choked and wanted to tell him he'd got it wrong but they both knew he'd read her exactly right. It was disconcerting. It felt dangerous, that with him she might be an open book when she'd spent so many years cultivating an impenetrable veneer of calm, capable self-sufficiency.

It was also strangely exhilarating, the feeling that here was a man who could get into her head with such ease. The desire winding down her spine increased another degree, further outweighing the anxiety in her belly.

'Which voice won? The devil urging you, telling you it's just dinner, or the angel warning you against it?'

And suddenly dangerous and exhilarating were ever so much more appealing than safe and capable. The devil she could cope with. It was when Ned's voice, with its deep, treacled tones, rich with entreaty, was added into the equation that she thought, To hell with it. It would only be one date, the devil whispered, as the angel all but gave up on her.

A date with the devil?

Her gaze met his with magnet-like force and the area around them seemed to shrink in contrast to the power of his presence. And in that moment, she knew that so long as the devil had green eyes like Ned's, there was not a woman alive whose angelic tendencies had any hope of shouting down that other, darker voice.

Her angel gave it one last shot. 'I only have one ticket.'

'Do you always play by the rules?'

'I guess so.' A brief, thrilling flare lit inside her. Safe Sarah aimed the extinguisher at it and said instead, 'Besides, you'd probably find it very dull and dry.'

'I think there'd be ways of livening the evening up. Women in evening gowns, all trying to outshine one another, a bit of dancing. There's always fun to be had.'

Spurred on by the gleam in his eyes, she teetered very close to ignoring the rules. Her rules.

And she might have done it except that, at that moment, lights began flashing, bells started ringing and an announcement came over the PA system ending all chance at having a conversation without yelling. Five seconds earlier she and Ned had had the place to themselves, or so it had seemed, but now there were firemen pouring into the area from all directions, running for the appliances. Before she'd had a chance to really process what was going on Ned had already bent to her side, pressed a feather-light kiss on her cheek and said, 'Gotta go, that's my crew being called. I'll be in touch.'

She stood still, transfixed, marvelling at the feel of Ned's lips on her skin. As light as the touch had been, it had held the promise of much, much more. She needed a moment to savour it and, besides, she wasn't leaving now, not when there was a full-scale response happening in front of her. She watched Ned kick off his shoes and in one movement step into a pair of overalls and boots. He pulled the overalls up over his dark pants, hoisting the straps over his shoulders. Seconds later, he was swinging up into the front passenger seat, his biceps bulging as he pulled his weight up. In less than a minute the appliance was pulling out of the station.

It took less time than that to burn a fabulous image of Ned the firefighter into her visual cortex, an image she just knew would be replayed over and over until she saw him again. Although she had a strong suspicion she'd spend as much time regretting that she'd also missed her chance to thumb her nose at convention and take him to the dinner after all.

As it was, once again she went to a five-star event on her own. And as she entered the foyer of the hotel, all dressed up but all alone, she knew what she really wanted was to walk in on the arm of a man with a twinkle in his eye and lips as soft as velvet.

CHAPTER THREE

SARAH stood to one side of the stage as the master of ceremonies gave his introductory spiel. Straightening her dress, she wished again she'd worn her fail-safe LBD instead of this uncharacteristic purchase. But somehow, when she'd gone shopping for shoes with her sister, she'd ended up buying the very bright ruby-red dress she was now wearing. Not for her sister's wedding, not for anything in particular and not even with this evening in mind.

Tori had convinced her to buy it. The task had been easy once Sarah had started to imagine what Ned would think if he ever saw her in this dress. A ridiculous reason and now she was paying the price.

Shot through with gold, the red silk shone in the lights, placing it in a different league to the sedate dresses she usually wore on such nights. From the audience's perspective she looked demure; the dress had long sleeves and a high, rounded neckline, but it was virtually backless and she was now feeling exposed. She had no problem being in the spotlight for her work or for her public speaking skills—it was what she did all day, every day and it came as naturally as breathing after all these years. But in this dress she suddenly felt like she would be stepping onto the stage as a woman with desires and sensuality, a woman who just happened to be a doctor, as opposed to a respected professional who just happened to be a woman.

It was only as a woman that she ever felt vulnerable.

She was the second of three speakers at the gala dinner for National Organ Donor Awareness Week. Representatives from two families were speaking. A donor family had preceded her and a recipient family was to follow. Her speech was from a medical perspective and she was intent on keeping any personal twist out of it. She had different speeches depending on the basis on which she'd been invited. Tonight she was here as a doctor, not as someone with a personal story.

She was here to deliver the facts and her speech was being videotaped and snippets would be shown on TV news programmes for the rest of the week. A less than perfect delivery was not an option.

With the MC's introduction over, Sarah stepped up to the microphone, checking the autocue was showing her speech and not somebody else's. She knew her speech by heart but wanted the autocue to hand, just in case.

She scanned the room, picking out a few spots in the crowd where she could focus her attention. The audience was attentive, watching her with anticipation. It was a group of the converted faithful after all, here because they were interested. There were some high-profile sports stars and media personalities in the audience who'd given their time and presence to promote awareness of the need for organ donations. Silently clearing her throat, she took a deep breath, found a few friendly faces and began, finding her natural rhythm as she progressed through her speech.

'This year alone there are over 1700 people waiting for donated organs. Without transplants, these people will continue to live restricted lives, lives ruled by medical appointments, medications and machines. That's assuming they are able to stay alive, because the harsh reality is, without organ donation, a number of these people won't make it at all. Every day is critical.

'There are over five million registered donors in Australia, almost a quarter of our population, but our current donor rate is point-zero-zero-one per cent.' She paused to let the figures register. 'So only *one* out of every *one hundred thousand* Australians actually becomes an organ donor. We have one of the lowest donor rates in the Western world.

'I know you are here tonight either because organ donation has affected you personally or because it is a cause you believe in. But our message this year is, please, do more than believe, make sure you register as a donor. And, please, encourage your family members to register too, talk about it together. If you can't bring yourself to register, discuss your feelings with your family so they are aware of your wishes.'

She went on to talk about a few specific, anonymous cases and saw plenty of people, men and women, with tears in their eyes. She'd managed to move them with her words and now hopefully, if they weren't donors already, they'd seriously consider registering.

'Confronting your own mortality is not easy and most of us do anything to avoid it. But we never know what is waiting for us around the corner. Take a moment now to look at the people around you.' Again, she waited while the room buzzed briefly, wondering where she was going.

'In a moment, in the not-too-distant future, one of you could find yourself depending for your very life on the incredible and brave gift of a perfect stranger. Or it might be your child's life that hangs in the balance as you watch the clock ticking inexorably on, praying and hoping against time for a miracle. The reverse side of that is that every one of you *also* has the power, through registering yourself as an organ donor, to be the maker of miracles.

'In this room tonight I know there are a number of people who wouldn't be alive if not for a successful transplant. You might well be sitting next to someone whose life has been saved in this way.' The room was perfectly still and quiet, but people were flicking glances about them, wondering if they were, in fact, sitting next to a transplant recipient. She knew she was bordering on being sensationalist, but getting the audience to commit emotionally to her topic was the very best guarantee they would change their behaviour once they left here tonight. She leant towards the microphone a touch. 'Those people are most likely only with us now because of the gift of a perfect stranger. Because of that gift, they have a whole life to live. And each time this happens, that gift gives entire families their lives back to them whole, too.'

Wrapping up her speech with an entreaty to take the information that had been placed on their tables and take action to register, Sarah left the stage to resounding applause, wishing her sister Tori was with her tonight. Sometimes they came together, sometimes Tori spoke instead of Sarah, sometimes they both did, but Tori was better at delivering the personal story and Sarah the medical perspective. Either way, it was always nice to have a familiar face to share the adrenalin rush of public speaking with afterwards.

Hovering out of sight at the side of the stage, Sarah stood in the shadows to watch the next speaker, not yet ready to slip back to her seat.

As her heart rate settled she became aware she was under scrutiny. Shrugging off the idea as nothing more than some guy ogling her because of her skin-tight red dress, she stayed focused on the speaker, choosing to ignore the sensation and hoping they'd grow tired of the view. But when the speaker had finished Sarah could still feel someone's eyes on her.

She turned. The 'gentleman' in question was seated at a nearby table and, judging by the stains on his teeth, it looked as though he had a few too many glasses of red wine under his belt. Sarah watched, horrified, as their gazes met and the man lurched from his chair and began to weave a path towards her.

Once he reached her she'd be trapped between the stage stairs and the back wall and, while she was well able to get rid of unwanted attention, she'd really rather not have to deal with it. He was intruding on her high, the high she got from delivering a good speech, the high she got when she was reminded that, thanks to organ donation, her family was intact.

Could she dash up the steps and across the stage? It only took a glance to see that wasn't an option—the band was returning to their instruments and she'd be in their way.

She swept her gaze back across the tables.

And then she saw him.

Leaning against the bar at the side of the room, impeccable in a perfectly tailored dark suit, was Ned.

Correction. Leaning against the bar, looking immaculate *and* watching her with an appreciative look in his green eyes. Was that a sparkle of amusement as well as he watched her predicament?

She sent a half-smile his way before checking on the lecherous diner's progress—how much time did she have left to escape? Her chances of avoiding him were increasing as more people were moving about, heading for the dance floor. Perhaps she'd be able to melt into the crowd. Perhaps she'd be able to reappear by Ned's side.

Mr Lecherous had been waylaid but he was still looking her way.

She glanced back at Ned.

He was gone.

Enough was enough.

He'd watched her being targeted by the old drunk guy. OK, not that old, and maybe not even that drunk, but definitely undesirable. Initially he'd found it interesting, curious to see how Sarah would handle it. She wasn't in any danger and he didn't imagine she'd lack the confidence to tell the bloke to take a hike. In fact, he was looking forward to witnessing that. He'd derive great satisfaction from watching another guy crash and burn before he tested his own style of charm on her.

But now she'd seen him.

She'd seen him and smiled.

Now he didn't want to sit back and wait. He wanted to get what he'd come for, and that was her.

He wanted to get to know her better.

He wanted to see what she was like away from work.

And if his luck was in, he wanted to see if she tasted as good as she looked in that red dress.

A dress like that should be illegal. A dress like that was just asking to be taken off. By him.

He made short work of the distance between them. Then he was by her side, a second before the competition arrived at a stumble. Satisfaction swelled through him when Sarah didn't even appear to notice his competitor's unsteady arrival. As soon as she saw Ned, her face lit up with a smile that was all for him.

And when he held out his hand, she didn't hesitate before stepping into the circle of his arm. She was tucked against him as she asked, 'What are you doing here?'

'You wanted to know what was under this fireman's uniform.' He bent his head to speak softly in her ear, and was rewarded as a small sigh escaped her full lips, painted to match her dress. 'I thought it best to show you.'

She looked down the length of him, slowly, almost like a caress, and the movement caused an involuntary clenching in his groin before she brought her gaze back to meet his. 'A tuxedo?' There was amusement in her eyes but there was also appreciation. It was appreciation that he returned in full.

'A tuxedo,' he agreed, 'and a pressing need to twirl a beautiful woman around the dance floor.'

He slid his fingers down her arm before taking her

by the hand and leading her onto the dance floor for the moment of truth.

If the chemistry he was sure they had truly existed, the dance floor was the place to reveal it—it was the universal leveller. Women usually made their desire for him plain. Sarah hadn't done that. She'd given off hints aplenty but she'd also played it safe. Very safe.

But now there was no place to hide.

Now he'd see if she was as comfortable in that crazy red dress as she looked or whether she was playing dress-up.

He'd see if the signals of interest she'd conveyed were real or whether she'd run scared, afraid of exploring desire.

The band was playing a salsa and as they arrived on the dance floor they fell into step. She could dance, that much he could tell immediately; she knew how to follow his lead. He slipped his hand around to the small of her back, felt her skin beneath his fingers and felt her tense momentarily, but as the music swelled around them, he felt her body relax. He resisted the temptation to run his hand up her bare back and concentrated instead on the music.

Sarah was the perfect size to partner him. Small and slight, she floated across the floor. Her scent swirled around him too as he spun her round, floral notes enveloping him as the five hundred other people in the room receded into the darkness. He guided her back in to him and they moved across the floor, dancing with an ease that belied the fact this was their first time together.

What was that old joke about banning sex because it might lead to dancing?

If this was how they danced together…

The music built to a crescendo and they increased pace a touch. Sarah's cheeks were flushed, both of them were breathing rapidly, and her pupils were inky and large.

Inviting.

Suggestive.

Available?

One way to find out. As the music ended, she stayed in his arms, stayed exactly where she'd been, and made no move to break the contact.

He'd been right about her. She moved like someone who knew what she was doing. 'The lady can dance.'

'So can the firefighter. Which are you, a dancer or a fighter?'

'I think that should be, a lover or a fighter?' He let the correction, full of suggestion, sink in for a moment and he knew the instant Sarah registered the invitation.

Her eyes widened and she looked fleetingly embarrassed. But it was only for a moment and then her smile turned into a laugh and she said, 'You've just given yourself away. You're no Casanova, you're a shocker so you must be a firie through and through.'

'Is that good? Or bad?' He dropped his voice to show her that in his view being bad was very, very good.

She'd pegged him as a charming playboy and, if she were sensible, now she had firm proof, she'd let that serve as a timely warning and run.

Instead, the warm glow that had started spreading through her the moment she'd seen him tonight became even more delicious as he flirted with her.

So without the need for further discussion she let him lead her out of the function room to the small bar area. It felt so right to have him here, to have his hand on her waist helping her onto the barstool—and, embarrassingly, in this mad-fool dress, she actually needed the help—and then she remembered.

She still had no idea why he *was* here.

But while his hands were still at her waist, while she could still feel the touch of his fingers on her skin, the shivers of anticipation meant she couldn't speak.

'Champagne?' he asked.

Sarah nodded her reply and waited until he'd been served and had placed her drink before fishing for an answer to her earlier question.

'I obviously got it wrong when I told you tonight's been sold out for ages.'

'No, you were right.'

'So how *did* you get your tickets?'

'My mother books a table every year, but she's overseas at the moment so I said I'd take it for her. The fire department donates prizes for the silent auction so the guys were happy to support the cause.'

She nodded. 'I saw the prizes. Impressive.'

'Did you bid on any?'

'Quite a few.'

'The date with our Bachelor of the Year? That's always popular.'

Sarah sipped her champagne and wrinkled her nose as a rush of bubbles tickled her face and an idea sprang to mind. 'That's not *you*, is it?'

He laughed and shook his head. 'Not this year.' Loosening his bow-tie until it hung lazily around the collar of his white shirt, he fixed her with a penetrating look and asked, 'If I was, what would you have bid?'

Not 'would you have bid,' she noticed, but '*what* would you have bid'.

'If it came with a guarantee of a dance, I'd have maxed out my credit card.' Returning his look with one that was equally full of confidence and innuendo, she lowered her lashes then looked back at him with eyes now full of disingenuous entreaty. 'I'm a soft touch when it comes to charity.' Maybe it was her dress, maybe it was Ned or maybe together the two made for a potent combination because she couldn't quite believe how free she felt to flirt. And so gorgeous was the sensation she was almost able to convince herself that the anxiety born of her self-consciousness was nowhere to be seen.

Who said she couldn't flirt without it being a promise of something more? Wasn't that the definition of flirting? Ned looked like he might have memorised the thesaurus on the subject.

'If you knew you were coming tonight, why didn't you tell me?'

'Because it was more fun watching you make excuses about why you couldn't invite me.'

'That's mean.' But she was laughing, too. How could she not when his enjoyment was so genuine?

'And,' he added, 'I thought it would be fun to surprise you.'

'Was it?'

'Very,' he said, his voice a relaxed drawl.

'What if you hadn't found me?'

'You wally,' he said, using the Australian expression

that, curiously, made her feel even more familiar with him, as if he was terribly fond of her instead of hardly knowing her at all. 'You were speaking. All I had to do was look up on stage.'

'Ah, yes. There is that.'

'Besides…' She waited for him to fill in the silence. 'You outshine every woman here tonight.' The teasing note had gone from his voice now and it didn't occur to her to dismiss his comments as pure flattery. She was under his spell, pure and simple. 'And there's not a man here who hasn't noticed.'

Now he had her. And it felt wonderful. In the face of a compliment of that magnitude, her power of speech deserted her. She'd been kidding herself she was just having fun. One sincere word of praise from him and she'd gone to mush.

'I was right,' she said as he raised an eyebrow and leant back on his stool. 'You are shockingly charming.' But she couldn't muster much objection when it was an effort to swallow and not reveal how tingly his comments had left her. And, besides, why would a girl object when she was loving every minute of being the centre of his attention?

He touched his temple in salute. 'Born to the trade. So, now you know why I'm here, I think you should tell me how you got involved with the foundation.'

And just like that, the delectable bubble in which she'd been floating burst and agonising self-consciousness returned. Because the reason she was here was inextricably linked to the reason, via the disastrous conduit of her ex-boyfriend, she avoided relationships. Or, rather, why she avoided anything that might lead to physical intimacy.

She couldn't believe she'd let herself drift about in a heady cloud of sexual desire, tempted by the idea she had the choice to act on that feeling and sleep with Ned. She spluttered as she took another sip of champagne.

'OK?'

She nodded but she was far from OK.

'Are you sure? You looked upset.'

'Sure as sure.' She took another sip of champagne, proving to him, to her, she was fine. 'I'm here as a doctor. I get asked to speak at these events.' That was true. Ned didn't need to know it was only part of the truth.

His eyes were narrowed, he was scrutinising her face, but he didn't challenge her answer, didn't press her for more information. Seamlessly, he moved the conversation on, smooth as smooth, chatting to her about his day, about a couple of funny incidents, taking the focus off her until once again she relaxed and started chatting, too, filling him in on the mysteries of life in a busy hospital department.

The guy had some sort of magic mixed in his blood because she swore it only took a matter of minutes before the rush of attraction that drowned out common sense was back.

'Chatting with you makes a nice change from having women ask me how I slide down poles.'

Now she didn't know which way to look. 'They don't?'

'Actually, they do, all the time.' He laughed and she fell just a little more inextricably under his spell. All she could think about was how the white of his dinner shirt set off the olive accents of his skin, and how the green of his eyes stood out so beautifully against the simplicity of the whole black and white tuxedo look. And how well he filled out that tuxedo…

'But what I mean is, it's nice to have a proper conversation, not just silly stuff.' He took her hand in his and thoughts of how he filled out his tuxedo were bumped aside. All she could think of was how she'd never, ever had such an overwhelming desire to have a man kiss her. To have a man do anything at all. 'Sarah, I've enjoyed your company…'

Was there a 'but' coming? Was he about to make a run for it, right in the middle of her fantasies of making love with him? If it was, she was ready to shrivel up on the spot with mortification.

'You're looking worried,' he interrupted himself. 'And here I was hoping you wouldn't be able to refuse my dinner invitation. I'm pretty sure I haven't read the signs wrong.'

His tone and the way his mouth tilted up at one corner said he didn't believe he'd done that for a second. And it also convinced her that he wasn't looking for a way out.

'Dinner?'

'Dinner. You. Me. Some food. Some wine. Or me, you, some wine, some food. The order we can play with as long as the basic ingredients are there.'

'You. Me. Dinner,' she repeated. Her hand was still in his and now he was shaking hers, his grip firm and lovely. A grip that said he was in control, he could be trusted.

Flirting was OK, right? Dinner was OK? She ignored the thought that she was rewriting her rule book with every passing second in this man's company. Ignored the fact that she was far too aware of him and should be keeping her distance.

'Deal.' The shiver of awareness was back, racing through her, wreaking havoc on her equilibrium.

Me and Ned equals serious risk of making a fool of myself any minute, was the warning flashing through her mind. And if monosyllables were all she'd been reduced to, the safest option was to go home. Now. Before her mind turned to total jelly beneath the on-slaught of her desire and, against her better judgement, she ended up in bed with him tonight.

Some time in the past week she seemed to have for-gotten her vow of abstinence. The attraction she felt was so powerful it was dangerous and she needed to get some distance and some perspective.

There was a tiny smile flirting with the corner of his lips, as if he knew exactly where her thoughts were taking her: the bedroom.

She smiled back, unable to resist, before delivering her exit speech. 'Dinner would be lovely but now I'd better grab a taxi. I'm working tomorrow.' Somehow her sense of self-preservation had kicked in and, not only did she manage to excuse herself, she actually started to climb down from her stool.

Immediately, Ned let go of her hand to help her down. 'I'll walk you downstairs. Did you bring a coat?'

He stayed close beside her as she collected her coat from the cloakroom and she was as aware of his presence as if she were still in his arms.

Taking her coat from her, he helped her into it and she felt a pang of regret he wasn't trying to convince her to stay longer. Instinctively, though, she knew a man like Ned didn't have to convince a woman to do anything. He just had to look at them as he was looking at her right now, like she was the only one in the room, and women would be eating out of his hand.

He wrapped the coat around her shoulders and his fingers brushed her skin and lingered. She knew his touch was deliberate and the pang of regret disappeared, the air around them electrified as though the heat they were generating had energy to spare. He adjusted the collar for her and stayed close, his hand skimming her lower back as they made their way from the mezzanine down to the hotel foyer where he asked the concierge to call her a cab before leading her towards a cluster of lounges beside the front windows. The hotel doors opened, letting in a blast of cool air that sliced at her bare ankles, making her shiver at the sudden change in temperature.

'Cold?' Ned didn't wait for her answer before wrapping one arm around her shoulders, pulling her against his chest, enveloping her in his warmth. She didn't resist his gesture. Why would she? It was so comfortable, so natural, to be held by him. If he thought she was cold, she wasn't going to argue.

She closed her eyes and concentrated on Ned's heartbeat, pulsing through the thin fabric of his shirt. His chest was firm beneath her cheek and his hip pressed against hers as she slipped her arms around his back and underneath his dinner jacket.

'Sarah?'

She heard him whisper her name. She opened her eyes and looked up at him. His green eyes were darker now, his gaze intense as he watched her. In slow motion she saw him bend his head towards her, his eyes fixed on her lips. He was going to kiss her and she wanted him to, wanted it more than she should. She knew it would be her undoing. Something told her one kiss would never be enough, but she was powerless to stop him and she knew she wasn't about to try.

She kept her face tilted up, watching him, only closing her eyes at the last second as she felt the first touch of his lips.

And what lips... Thoughts drifted seamlessly away, words she tried to form to capture the feel of him blended into nothingness. The most she was cognisant of was everything other than them had ceased to matter. Was the world still even there?

Everything in her mind shifted naturally into a shapeless awareness of warm and wonderful sensations, melting her bones and sending sparks through every vein.

He brushed across her mouth so gently she could have been dreaming.

But it wasn't a dream and her body knew it, though her mind was unable to process the magnificence of how he made her feel.

Lips parting, his kiss deepened, and the heat that washed over her was like a cocoon.

Warm, sweet, tender.

Magnificent.

And all for her.

One minute, ten minutes. It didn't matter, no length of time would be enough.

It was the perfect kiss—tender yet passionate, gentle but firm, sensitive and all-encompassing. But it was more than just a kiss.

The sounds of a Saturday night in the city—the honking of horns, the blare of car stereos, the occasional backfiring exhaust—receded into a dim corner of her mind. There was only room for the sensations of soft against hard, warm against cool, rough against smooth, the awareness of his scent, impossibly intoxicating and wiping out all coherent thoughts.

Except one.

The kiss was perfect.

He was perfect.

And it was only when the concierge interrupted with a discreet cough to announce the arrival of her taxi that other thoughts rudely returned. Side by side but not touching, they left the hotel. Ned helped her into the taxi and she was being driven away before she remembered the problem with what had just happened.

Ned might well be perfect. He might even think she was worth his interest.

But thanks to her ex, she knew it would all come unstuck. Thanks to Alistair, she knew exactly how far from perfect she was. And if she gave in to her growing desire and slept with Ned, that was almost guaranteed to end it with him straight away.

If Alistair, with so many of his own failings, hadn't been able to see past her flaws, visible and invisible, how would someone as perfect as Ned ever want her?

By mid-morning Sunday, Sarah had jumped with nervous anticipation three times in response to the scream of sirens as emergency services vehicles had raced along the arterial road near the inner-city home she shared with her sister. It didn't seem to matter what sort of help was on its way, her body was apparently primed to respond to the sirens of ambulances, police cars and fire engines. Three sirens and three times she'd all but leapt to attention, an immediate image of Ned cued by the sound of any approaching wail.

It was also an abundance of images of Ned that had caused sleep to come slowly last night, teasing her mind and body awake each time her eyelids had fluttered closed. And the minute she had woken up, reality had clawed at her with sharp nails, reminding her that if she indulged her desires, she'd leave herself open to being rejected. If it had hurt with Alistair, how much more would it hurt with Ned?

Still, her fears hadn't been enough to stop her dreams of lips teasing and hands moving over warm bodies.

Common sense told her to forget it all. The best way to avoid rejection was to avoid men. But Ned was a positive to her negative and the strong attraction was difficult to deny, especially as she knew he felt it, too. Adding to her confusion was the knowledge that if he walked through the front door this minute, her legs would probably buckle instead of bearing her weight and the only words she'd rustle up would be akin to begging for more of last night rather than 'no'.

She was simultaneously mulling over her predicament and putting away the last of the dishes when Tori ambled into the kitchen.

Her identical twin sister, younger by a few minutes, was resplendent in a slip of a negligee and enormous pink fluffy slippers in the shape of teddy bear heads. With its plunging neckline, her attire was hardly decent by anyone's standards and a single glance before Tori turned to the fridge was all Sarah needed to take her mind straight back to her own problems.

On Tori, the negligee revealed more than it would on most women: straight between her half-visible breasts ran a dark scar which disappeared into the silk folds of her nightie like a road disappearing over the horizon. It was a very clear reminder to Sarah of what was at stake and of why she couldn't afford to get too close to Ned.

'Got a minute?' Tori was asking as she yanked open the fridge and stood looking, apparently waiting for food to introduce itself to her. 'I want to talk to you about something.'

'Shoes, dress, entrées or invitations?' Sarah shook off her own problems and thoughts about scars. She was driving herself crazy, going around in circles. 'What kept you up last night? Sometimes I wonder how you made the one really hard decision on your own.' In answer to Tori's look of query, she added, 'Who you were going to marry.'

'Harry was the easy part,' she said as she finally extracted an apple and sank her teeth into it. Between bites she added, 'I've never had a single doubt on that score. Besides, ye of little faith, it's nothing to do with Harry. It's not even about the wedding.' Intrigued, Sarah had to wait until Tori took a few more bites from her apple, making her wonder if she was deliberately delaying. 'I'm going to contact my organ donor's family and I want to know if you want to do the same.'

It took Sarah a few seconds to work out what Tori had just said. 'That was out of left field.'

'You don't think it's a good idea?' Tori was watching her closely and Sarah knew her sister was reading her for any indication she thought the idea was rotten.

'It's not that, but you've always said you didn't need to know—why now?'

Tori nodded emphatically, her dark hair, a shorter version of Sarah's, bobbing in waves about her face. 'It didn't start playing on my mind until knew I was getting married.'

Ah, so there was a tenuous link to the wedding. But what else lay behind Tori's sudden announcement?

'What difference does your wedding make?'

'If it wasn't for my transplant, I wouldn't be here today and I most definitely wouldn't be getting married. That's worth a thank-you note and right now seems like the time, when I'm about to start the rest of my life with the man of my dreams.' She underlined her words with a long sigh to make her point. 'I've given my heart to Harry but I'm more aware than ever that it was someone else's heart before.'

'Don't you think you've left it a bit late if you want to thank them before the wedding?'

Tori shook her head. 'My wedding's the reason I want to find the family but it's not a deadline. It doesn't matter if I don't find out until later but I want to start the process now. Besides, working at the foundation, I'm hoping I can pull a few strings and speed things up a bit. I thought if I'm trying to find my family, you might want to do the same. It might feel weird if one of us finds out and the other one doesn't.'

'That's assuming I want to know.'

'Don't you?'

'I'm not sure.' Sarah didn't think she wanted to go down that path but she also didn't want to try to explain her feelings right now. 'Let me ask you something—

what if your donor family doesn't want any contact? What then?'

Tori shrugged, aiming her apple core at the compost container on the kitchen bench and scoring a goal. 'Even if they don't, I can still write and thank them. They don't have to respond.' She slid off the table, saying over her shoulder as she stepped into the bathroom adjacent to the kitchen, 'I'm having a shower and after that I'm writing to the foundation. Are you going to do it, too?'

Would she?

Tori closed the bathroom door and Sarah slipped a finger inside her T-shirt and traced the skin there. A scar separated her breasts in exactly the same place as Tori's.

Tori didn't give two hoots about her scar, she never had. Yet for Sarah, it played a large part in defining who she was. It wasn't as easy as wishing she could ignore it. She'd tried that. She couldn't blame Alistair completely, although he had certainly been responsible for stripping away the last vestiges of her confidence with his insidious belittling treatment of her when she had been too young to see what he had been doing.

He was out of her life now and thoughts of him were irrelevant except for his lasting legacy: she'd vowed never to be vulnerable again. And she'd been doing admirably until Ned.

She ran her finger over the scar again. Did she want to know whose heart lay behind it?

Or was the answer simply that it was her heart now?

She knew better than to think it was that simple. Nothing was—at least, not when other people entered into the equation. She'd felt the effects of that single point of difference all her life. Beyond the looks and the questions, many people saw a 'sideshow' sign flashing above her head—the scar, the idea of the surgery involved, the continuing need for medication and another person's heart beating inside her chest. It was too much for some people, and others had over the years thrown it in her face. None more than Alistair.

Which was why, although she could never get away from her reality, she did have control over one thing: who she let close and how close she let them.

So while she'd started the morning with one burning question, now she had two: should she give in to desire and deal with the humiliation afterwards?

And did she really want to know whose heart it was that was both her greatest gift and the greatest complicating factor in her life?

CHAPTER FOUR

SARAH had spent three days alternating between a delirious haze, accompanied by visions of Ned, and worry over whether she'd now hear back from the foundation since she'd taken the step of writing. By Wednesday morning, when Ned appeared to have vanished from the face of the earth, she was left with only the worry. And feeling, in turns, cross and foolish.

The reality was he'd kissed her once and had not been seen since.

Why hadn't he rung?

Her home number was unlisted but he knew where she worked.

Stop it! she chastised herself for the hundredth time. She was going to make herself crazy if she didn't find a suitable distraction and the emergency department being unusually quiet for the past couple of days wasn't helping her cause.

She checked the triage board—only two names were on it and she wasn't the attending doctor for either of them. Glancing at the waiting area again, she saw the chairs remained as empty as they'd been all morning.

Her mobile phoned beeped with a message received and she snatched it up, eager for the distraction. It was Tori.

'Hav delivrd both ltrs to Org Fnd, fingers xx we get news soon.'

Predictably, Tori had launched straight into her latest project and had carried Sarah along with her. Sarah had agreed to write to the foundation, expressing interest in contacting her donor family, to keep Tori off her case. Quite the opposite of Tori, Sarah crossed her fingers that the donor family wouldn't want contact.

She was still standing in the middle of the room, lost in her thoughts, when she saw the triage sister beckoning her to the desk. Lilli was on the phone and Sarah headed across, hanging over the counter as she waited for the other woman to finish the call. Hopefully something was coming in that would distract her from all her issues.

'There's been a fire at one of the backpacker hostels,' Lilli told her. 'Two casualties coming in.'

Ned?

It was his station that would respond to any inner-city fires. Her mouth was suddenly dry and it was with difficulty she asked, 'Did you get any names?'

Lilli shook her head. 'Just injuries. Two civilians with burns and smoke inhalation.'

Sarah released the breath she'd been holding and started preparing to receive the victims. Civilians. Not Ned. The fingers of fear that had gripped her heart relaxed their hold.

They were starting to win the battle now. There were four appliances at the scene and the crews had managed to contain the blaze and stop it from spreading to neighbouring buildings. But the old two-storey structure that was the backpacker hostel was still burning fiercely.

Ned emerged from the building where he had been conducting a search and rescue. It was a slow process in a fire like this. No one knew how many people had been inside to begin with and, at half past eight in the morning, there was no way of knowing which backpackers had already left for the day and who was still out from the night before. The only way of knowing if the building was empty was to check every room.

Having to come out of the building every ten minutes to change his oxygen cylinder didn't help to speed up the process. There was a fair bit of action as guys came in and out of the building to change their BA tanks, replenish their oxygen and hand over their tags. Ned was hanging his tag on the control board so Simmo, the guy in charge of monitoring everyone on BA, would know he'd gone back inside, when an alarm grabbed his attention. It was loud and getting louder with each beep.

Ned knew immediately what it was. A motion detector alarm was fitted to each breathing apparatus kit worn by the firies and set to activate if the person wearing it hadn't moved for thirty seconds. These alarms usually turned out to be false and the alarm would just be reset. But if a crew member was down, time was of the essence.

He checked the board beside Simmo to see whose alarm was sending out the signal. According to the board, the alarm was attached to Jake.

'Appliance 201 to all portable units. Please confirm your status. Portable 201, Jake, do you read me? Over,'

Simmo called over the two-way radio. Ned waited for a response as the alarm continued to beep.

Alex, Tony and Paul all checked in and were accounted for but there was still no reply from Jake. The alarm was still beeping and they could only assume Jake was unconscious. If he was trapped and immobilised he'd leave the alarm on so he could be located, but if he was conscious he would have been in radio contact by now.

Ned knew Jake had been searching in the north-eastern corner of the building on the second floor. He knew where to start looking.

He told the incident controller where he was heading and raced back into the burning building. He had ten minutes of oxygen, but he had to hope he found Jake before that. Jake didn't have ten minutes to spare.

The temperature inside was incredible. The heat on its own was exhausting but the humidity and the steam caused by the huge amounts of water being pumped onto the flames created additional stress. Ned entered through the front door on the south side of the building and tried to keep as low to the floor as possible as he raced for the stairwell on the eastern wall. He concentrated on keeping his breathing even and controlled. Jake would need to share his oxygen when he found him and he wanted to have some in reserve.

He followed the passage around to his left. Visibility was only a few feet but thankfully the corridor had remained relatively clear. He pulled open the stairwell door and almost fell over Jake.

He quickly checked the area around Jake, looking for hazards. He could hear Jake breathing—the distinctive click of the breathing apparatus indicated all was OK there. Jake's right foot was at a strange angle and Ned guessed he'd broken his ankle but he wasn't sure if Jake had other injuries as well. He shook Jake's shoulder gently and Jake opened his eyes.

Ned put his thumb and forefinger together, making a circle, asking if everything was OK. Jake pointed to his right ankle and Ned nodded. Jake moved his left leg and left arm, indicating all his other joints were working and Ned took that as meaning Jake hadn't suffered a spinal injury. His alarm was still beeping. Ned had left it on to give the others time to find them if need be, but now he knew he could safely move Jake he turned it off.

He helped Jake up, getting him onto his left foot, well aware the movement could make Jake pass out again, knowing he only had a few seconds to get him over his shoulder. Jake was solidly built but the adrenalin coursing through Ned gave him extra strength. He felt Jake's deadweight over his shoulder as he got him into a fireman's lift and knew he'd lost consciousness again. At least that meant he didn't have to worry about hurting him further as he carried him out of the stairwell and out of the building.

Ned was aware of the cheers as they emerged from the hostel. The crowd of onlookers hadn't diminished and they craned their necks to see something, anything. Ned often thought they didn't mind whether they saw triumph or death—they just wanted to see some action. Even now, the crowd couldn't know whether Jake was dead or alive but still they cheered.

Ned ignored them, taking Jake to the waiting paramedics. He put Jake onto the stretcher and stripped off his own helmet and mask.

'He's got a busted ankle but doesn't appear to have any other injuries. He regained consciousness briefly,' Ned told the paramedics as they got to work.

The incident controller appeared beside him. 'The building's fully evacuated. Do you want to go to the hospital with Jake?'

Ned pulled off his BA, handing it to the IC, along with his helmet. 'No worries. I'll call you from there.' He waited as the stretcher was slid into the back of the ambulance before jumping into the front passenger seat. The adrenalin was still flowing but now it was mixed with relief.

'Sarah, another ambulance is on its way from the fire,' Lilli called out as she reappeared from the treatment rooms, having stabilised the backpacker suffering from smoke inhalation. 'It's a firie this time. Do you want to take it?'

That squeeze of fear tightened around her heart again but she nodded, knowing she'd worry less once she knew who was injured. Her facade was as calm as ever but underneath a rising sense of dread was making her feel shaky.

The moment the ambulance pulled into the emergency bay, Sarah was ready, pulling open the doors with shaking hands, looking straight at the fireman's face as she listened to the paramedic's summary.

It wasn't Ned. The tension in her chest abated but her hands still shook a little as she helped to pull the stretcher from the ambulance. Backing away, she heard a familiar voice.

'Hello, Sarah.'

On the opposite side of the stretcher, Ned had appeared.

Sarah had never been so pleased to see anyone. He was safe. And he was here. Every cross thought she'd had about him not calling evaporated in an instant. Her worry that he'd already forgotten he'd kissed her vanished in the same instant. He was sweaty and dirty, his thick, fire-resistant overalls were filthy and he smelt overwhelmingly of smoke, but he was the best thing she'd seen in days.

And it wasn't just relief. Despite his unkempt appearance, he still sent her libido on a trip to the moon. His tousled, untidy look filled her head with visions of him climbing out of bed. Her bed.

He nodded a greeting at her, a half-smile of acknowledgement on his face but totally professional. 'This is Jake, he's on my crew.'

Right, Jake, the injured fireman. That's what she needed to focus on. She returned his nod and looked down at the stretcher, away from Ned. With her heart hammering in her chest, she made herself focus on getting her patient inside, gripping the stretcher to start pushing it towards the hospital even though all she wanted was to reach out and touch Ned, to make sure he was really there and unharmed.

They entered through the emergency doors and Ned stepped away. He was leaving already?

'I'll wait here. You'll let me know how he is?'

'Sure,' she said, not caring how big her smile was now she knew he was sticking around.

It didn't take long to establish Jake's injuries weren't major. He'd sustained a fractured tibia when he'd missed a step and fallen down the stairs. He didn't appear to be suffering from concussion. He said he'd passed out from pain, so she prescribed some pain relief to tide him over while they waited for the portable X-ray machine. Then she left him under the care of the nurses while she went in search of Ned, willing herself to walk at an appropriate pace and not skid to a halt by his side in her haste to get back to him.

He was in the waiting area, pacing, and she knew immediately he wouldn't sit down, he'd consider himself too dirty. She could see, though, there were now some clean patches of skin showing through on his face so he must have splashed his face in the bathroom. As he turned and saw her, he quickened his step, reaching out to touch her on the arm, concern for his team member evident in his demeanour.

'Is he OK?'

'He'll be fine. I'm just waiting for the X-ray but it looks like he's only got a broken ankle. Jake told me you found him, carried him out of the building. You weren't hurt?'

'I'm tougher than that.' His concern had ebbed with her news and now his dimple flashed in his right cheek.

The tremble in her belly told her she was like every other female faced with a guy in uniform—and what hope was there when the guy in front of her filled out his uniform as finely as Ned? But though the sight of Ned in his uniform turned her on, the thought of him being in danger did not.

Then again…the image of Ned hauling the giant hoses into an inferno, dodging falling timbers, carrying someone—her!—to safety from the smoking rubble released another burst of adrenalin through her body.

'Although,' he continued, 'I prefer rescuing damsels in distress rather than big lugs like Jake.'

Damsels. Plural. That's what was wrong with her fantasy. It wouldn't be her he was carrying from a fire, it would be other women. And she could just imagine how those damsels would feel if Ned came to their aid. There were probably even women who'd walk *into* a burning building if it meant being carried back out again pressed close to Ned.

'Dr Richardson?' Sarah turned to find the radiographer behind her. 'The X-rays are ready.'

She nodded then turned back to Ned, not wanting this chance encounter to end. 'Can you wait a bit longer? I'll be back.'

'Sure.'

Sarah returned to the treatment cubicle to find Jake's fracture was more complicated than she'd expected. He needed surgery and that meant an ortho consult, which meant she could hand over his care and return to Ned. She refrained from saying 'Yippee' at the turn of events. She'd have to have a good long think about Ned's effect on her—he turned up at the department and she'd been having one uncharacteristic, unprofessional thought after another. At least she wasn't cutting corners with her patients, but once again, she had to force herself to walk at her normal pace back to Ned.

His presence filled the waiting area. His energy and vitality were a stark contrast to the physically and often emotionally battered people she usually saw in Emergency and made him shine. He looked ready to take on the world, a quintessential hero. Strength emanated from him, a key quality to his attractiveness, and she could see it now he was in such a contrasting environment. He was perfect for the role of the knight in shining armour and, despite the trite nature of her imaginings, she could just picture him charging to the rescue. Banishing the ridiculous thought to the far recesses of her mind, she focused her attention on the flesh-and-blood Ned.

Now things had calmed down and the triage area was empty again, she had a few spare minutes. The perfect opportunity to find out what he'd been doing or, rather, why he hadn't been in touch.

'Have you been busy at work?' She reprimanded herself. She sounded desperate. She may as well have stamped 'Why haven't you called?' across her forehead. It shouldn't matter. But it did.

Then again, one flash of that smile he was responding with now, one glimpse of his dimple, and she was back under his spell. What was it about Ned that made her forget her need for self-preservation?

He shook his head. 'Not really.' Ouch. That hurt. He wasn't even going to pretend work had kept him away. What more did she need to strengthen her resolve to avoid him? 'But I have been flat out getting ready for this weekend.' Her humiliation eased a little, hoping he was going to tell her he'd wanted to call but had had too much on.

'What extreme sport is on the agenda this weekend?'

'Nothing that adventurous. A mate and I have made our first wine. It's ready for bottling and I've been getting everything together.'

'What sort of wine is it?'

'Pinot noir. Not my usual taste but Max convinced me.' He paused for a moment, mischief dancing in his eyes. 'It doesn't need as long in oak as some of the other varieties.' The corners of his eyes creased a second before his smile appeared. She hadn't known him long but she'd studied him enough to know those creases were a harbinger for a drop-dead smile and a light-hearted comment, usually cheeky. 'Less time in the barrel means we can drink it sooner. I was all for that.'

She laughed, shaking her head in mock admonishment. 'Patience is a virtue but not when it comes to wine?'

'Waiting for something doesn't necessarily make it better. Life's short. If I wait, I might miss out.'

Ned in a nutshell? She'd have to get to know him better to work that out. It wasn't going to happen today, though, her pager told her as it started beeping.

'Why don't you come with me?'

His invitation caught her off guard and she had the distinct impression it had done the same to him, but he continued warmly enough. 'Come up to the hills with me. We'll bottle the wine and then stay for dinner.'

'Is your wine decent?' She was laughing at him, trying not to look like she was taking any of it too seriously, a struggle when she wanted to squeal like a teenager at the invitation.

'Even if it's lousy, Phoebe and Max are great company and Phoebe happens to be a fabulous cook.'

'What will you contribute to the day if Max knows about wine and Phoebe does the food?'

'Scintillating conversation. I'll pick you up at ten. Come ready to be scintillated.'

'That's a high bar you've set.' She reached into her pocket to pull out a small notebook and a pen. She scribbled something on the page and tore it off, adding, 'I hope you perform under pressure.'

As she handed it to him, at the exact moment he took hold of the paper and their gazes met, she realised her double entendre. It was his turn to laugh at her now, teasingly, but he let the moment slide by without comment.

He glanced at the paper. 'I think this says Young Street but you have classic doctor's writing.'

'It does and I do, I admit it. Number twenty-six, opposite the old church.'

'Excellent.' She turned to go and he added in a quieter voice, 'Just so you know, I perform best under pressure.'

She flicked a glance back at him, raised an eyebrow to suggest she was not going to get involved in that discussion and made herself scarce, knowing she'd be replaying every delicious second of this conversation over and over until she saw him again.

CHAPTER FIVE

HE HADN'T known what his intentions had been when he'd invited Sarah up to the hills but now he could see his spontaneity had paid off. Sarah and Phoebe had gelled immediately and perhaps because of this easy familiarity Sarah was more relaxed than he'd ever seen her.

If he ignored the time when he'd kissed her. Then she'd had a gratifyingly bone-melting aura of relaxation. Today she had an easy warmth, no doubt helped by the genuine welcome from his friends. He and Max were working in one corner of the old barn, filling bottles with their home-made wine, a task repetitive enough to allow him to keep an eye on the woman who was becoming the subject of an unreasonable number of his thoughts. The two women were laughing as they pasted bottle after bottle with the labels Max and Ned had designed. Sarah's face was alight with enjoyment, her throat long and slender as she tipped her head back and laughed at something the heavily pregnant Phoebe had said. Slight and dark, Sarah radiated warm intellect softened by a caring nature. And he knew already about the passionate fire that simmered beneath the calm surface. He hadn't been able to get it out of his head.

'She's great, Ned,' said Max, interrupting his thoughts, 'but I'm wondering what she sees in you, buddy. She doesn't fit your typical mould of datable women.'

'Because?'

'She's a brunette for a start. And, among other things, she's intelligent, successful, over twenty years of age—' He broke off with an 'Oomph' as Ned socked him in the arm. 'She's settling-down material, not fling material. Normally you'd run for the hills if her bra wasn't bigger than her IQ, so what gives?'

Ned was somewhere between being amused by Max's observations and panicked that moments before he'd had similar thoughts himself. 'You're maligning me. I'm a legs man. Bra size doesn't interest me.'

'Yeah,' scoffed Max, 'and I'm not intending to drink a drop of this wine we've bottled today and pigs might fly. But absolute nonsense aside, you like her and a fling isn't going to give you what you think you want from her.'

He shot Ned a lazy grin then turned his attention to the women still chatting and working on the other side of the barn.

'Hey, you two,' called out Max, 'production's slowing up over there. A little less chat and a little more labelling.' He intercepted his wife's look and added, 'Don't give me that look. Being eight months pregnant is apparently no impediment to spending days and days shopping for baby things and that's a lot more arduous.' Glancing at Ned, he muttered, 'For me, anyway.'

'Not having regrets, are you, buddy?' Ned asked Max as the women went back to labelling, still talking nonstop at an impressive pace. Whatever hard time Max could dish up, Ned could match it.

'Only about buying my wife's story that a baby can't grow up to be a functional adult unless it starts life with a NASA-certified stroller, pram, cot, bassinet, baby sling and highchair, not to mention aerodynamic nappies with in-built tracking devices.'

'That bad, hey?' Ned whacked him on the shoulder in sympathy.

'Put it this way, the change table has more dials and flashing lights than my car.'

The women had wandered over in time to hear the conversation and Sarah caught Ned's eye and smiled at Max's complaints. One smile, and all thoughts of the utter craziness of having brought her here fled. One smile, and he mentally recalculated the short-term future with her to extend to the next fortnight.

'What he fails to mention,' said Phoebe, smiling sweetly at her husband, 'is he was the one who insisted we buy that change table. Even I didn't see the need for an inbuilt radio or whatever it has.'

'Boys and their toys,' said Sarah, 'My guess is after bottling, that's where we'll find them, playing with all the buttons on your baby gadgets.'

Phoebe giggled. 'Max already has them lined up in the baby's room ready to show Ned. Although that might be a hard nut to crack, you'd be the last person to be interested in baby paraphernalia, right, Ned? Besides, you'd need to date someone for more than five minutes to ever risk getting to that stage.'

Phoebe covered her mouth with her hand the moment she'd said the words, her look of mortification completing the uncomfortable faux pas. It was something she often teased him about, but she'd never intentionally do so in front of his date.

His glance flew automatically to Sarah, who was busying herself with looking anywhere but him.

Max stepped into the growing silence. 'That's enough teasing for today, you two. I tell you, Sarah,' he said, touching her on the arm and drawing her back in, 'the teasing that goes on around here is positively juvenile. You can imagine what it was like living with the two of them. They carry on like brother and sister.'

Ned sent silent thanks to Max for his save and was pleased to see Sarah's relaxed demeanour return. Had Phoebe's comment thrown her? Or was she just not interested in anything more than a fling anyway? Well, that suited him, it was what he wanted. Phoebe was right. It was exactly the way he was.

He only had flings. He'd planned on any fling with Sarah lasting beyond the average couple of nights, but beyond that there was nothing different about this situation than any of the others.

Why, then, was he finding it almost impossible to concentrate on a simple task like bottling wine just because Sarah was standing so close? Close enough he swore he could smell her scent even above the luscious berry smells of the wine permeating the air. His awareness of everything around him was heightened by her presence. Even while eating lunch together, just a quick snack of bread and cheese, he'd been distracted by the way her even white teeth had torn into the thick bread, how she'd chewed each mouthful with deliberation, how her throat had worked as she'd drunk deeply from a glass of water.

Thanks to Sarah, he now knew how appealing it could be when strands of a woman's hair tugged free from the restraints of a ponytail to brush over her cheeks, before she'd pushed them back behind her neat ears. Thanks to her, he'd learned a smudge of barn-dust across the bridge of a rather perfect female nose was, in fact, adorable. Thanks to her, he'd found listening to two women talk about emergency medical procedures, something he should have been expecting as Phoebe was both a paramedic and paediatrician, was, frankly, a turn-on. When was the last time he'd dated someone who was not only intelligent but had no shame about it?

And finally, thanks to her, there was a tightness in his jeans he wasn't keen to share with the world. Frankly, she was a work hazard. Too delectable, too delicious and far, far too clearly intent on watching him do his stuff, a fact he was really getting a kick out of.

So when Phoebe said she was exhausted and needed to lie down and Max said he'd head up with her and start dinner, he was more than happy to volunteer to finish off the job, provided Sarah would keep him company. There wasn't much left to do anyway—the last batch of wine had been labelled and it was all packed in boxes, except the couple of bottles left out for dinner. Ned and Max were most of the way through cleaning the apparatus, hosing it out and disinfecting it for what they intended to be an annual event. So now was exactly the time for a few moments alone.

The minute Max and Phoebe left, the strain of being

so intensely aware of Sarah and not being able to act on it followed them right out the door. The strain had departed, but not his awareness of her. She'd picked up a cloth and was taking over where Max had left off, except she was scrubbing with great concentration over and over a spot that Max had already left sparkling clean. So she was as distracted as he was.

A good sign.

He watched her as she worked with her back to him. A deliberate tactic, to buy some time? She had to be as aware as he was of the tension that had been mounting between them all afternoon. Her denim-clad backside was moving from side to side as she wiped. He found himself hoping it would be another good ten minutes before she realized the bench was already clean.

Eventually she turned and leant that same pert backside against the edge of the bench, catching him watching her. Her cheeks coloured but her voice was light as she said, 'Hey, not fair! You've been standing there doing nothing.'

'And whose fault do you think that is?' He took a couple of steps nearer until he was close enough to take her in his arms if he moved just a fraction more. The adrenalin kicked up a notch, warming his blood. This was where it got interesting, this dance around each other, knowing from the way they were both breathing faster exactly how this would end but not yet knowing who would make the next move. 'If there was anything remotely as interesting as you in this barn, I promise I would've been hard at work.'

She caught her breath and then caught her lower lip between her teeth and nibbled. It was the nibble that finished him off. Enough was enough and it was time he was the one nibbling on the fullness of that lower lip.

It was all she'd been thinking about since he'd picked her up seven hours ago. Actually, since he'd kissed her a week ago it was all she'd really been able to think about.

So when he moved towards her she was predestined to meet him halfway and there was no hesitation then, no doubts or fears or even conscious thought beyond *I want this, I need this.* Her eyelids closed, her mouth tilted up to find his mouth, or he tilted her face to his, she wasn't sure. It just all happened, effortlessly and, just like that, those incredible sensations of a week ago returned in a rush that had her knees buckling under her.

Feeling her need, he scooped her up, lifting her in arms so strong she felt weightless, and then she was perched on the edge of the table, exactly where she'd so diligently been scrubbing. They'd both known what was going to happen—this moment they were in now. She wanted it, she needed it and she also knew it was madness to have it. But offered the opportunity, her resistance never stood a chance.

And now thoughts of common-sense decisions, fears about the pain that would surely follow, simply disappeared in a puff of smoke. There was nothing except the two of them. The two of them and their mutual need for each other.

She opened her eyes and found him watching her. His hands were on her waist, large and firm and warm, and their breath was coming hard and fast. With his hair tousled, he looked like he'd just rolled out of bed.

He was just so darned beautiful. Beautiful and

gentle, his size making her feel safe with him. Knowing he saved lives daily didn't do much to dampen that feeling either. Her insecurities had kept her safe from hurt for six years but she wasn't at all sure her instincts for self-preservation were a match for the magnetic pull she felt towards Ned.

Could she *just this once* let desire rule her head and heart and allow herself one tiny glimpse of how life would be if it was perfect? If *she* was perfect?

She saw his green eyes darken with desire and she was amazed at how unself-conscious she felt as she returned his gaze. Yet what woman with red blood coursing through her veins would be able to resist temptation when it was presented as beautifully as this? Even if there were a thousand very compelling reasons why she should just run away.

She parted her knees, allowing him to stand between her thighs, and she could feel the hard outline of him through his jeans, making any statement about what he wanted unnecessary.

And then she couldn't wait any longer and she pulled his head down to hers again, her fingers burying themselves in his hair, unable to be still, her desperation to be close to him, to have more of him, impelling her to press her body hard against his. He responded by deepening the kiss, turning her insides into a pool of treacled deliciousness and compelling all blood to rush from her extremities to where it was really needed, leaving her toes strangely numb and her belly on fire.

Behind closed eyelids, all she could see were colours dancing to the thrum of the blood in her ears. All she could feel was his hair in soft tufts twisted in her fingers, twisting so hard it must be hurting him, but she couldn't stop. She needed this closeness. The mass of his body was warming her legs, and his torso tilted to fit the curves of her own as she raised her body to meet his. The gentle pressure of his strong hand as he eased her into him was exquisite, while his other hand knotted into her hair. But where she was being rough, he was gentle, and where she was wanting fast, he was holding her back, teasing her, going slowly. And it was driving her crazy. She'd never felt anything like this, this out-of-control urge to simply have him here, now, on this very table, if that was what it came to!

And then his hand was on her face, cupping it with infinite gentleness, and she heard one of them groan softly through their kiss. It must have been her, and his caress traced the outline of her jaw before running in a slow, mind-bending tease of a line down her neck.

It was only as he ran a finger under the collar of her shirt and down towards the first button that the blood in her abdomen rushed in a life-saving bolt back to her brain and the warning signals blared again. It took her so much by surprise that she actually jumped, pulling his hand away from her shirt and taking her lips from his in the same instant. The warmth and the exhilaration came crashing down about her as she sat embarrassed, contrite and utterly, utterly confused.

What on earth would he think of her now?

She'd acted like a prude of the highest order and she'd be lucky if he didn't drive her home right now.

'Hey.' He tilted her face to meet his and her panic eased as she saw the look in his eyes—concerned, tender, and not a bit like someone who was about to tell her to scat. 'You OK?' He touched the tip of her nose, just lightly, just once, but it was a gesture more gentle and genuine than she'd ever received from anyone else. His voice was husky and she could feel his arousal hadn't abated one jot, but he'd stopped. Just like that he'd stopped and now he wasn't pressuring her. He was, unbelievably, concerned about her.

Maybe this could work out after all?

If she could engineer a little more time to force her old fears into high-security lockdown for a night or two, if he was willing to give her another chance, she could have this magnificent man.

She nodded slowly in answer to his question. He'd given her the moment she'd needed. For the next little while, she'd pretend with every ounce she had that she was very much OK.

Men like Ned didn't come along every day. *Or ever*, she reminded herself.

She took a huge gulp of courage, locked her recalcitrant insecurities away and, taking advantage of the fact her fingers were still laced together at the back of his neck, pulled his head back down to hers and gave herself up to the intense pleasure of being kissed by Ned Kellaway.

Three hours later, the four of them sat content around the living room, appetites sated after a delicious dinner whipped up by Max under close supervision by Phoebe.

By contrast, Ned's appetite where Sarah was concerned was in danger of going into overdrive. When she'd pulled away in the barn, he'd felt the loss of her like a shock, and when she'd been the one to resume their kiss, he'd never been so surprised. He wasn't sure what had happened but he'd been careful to hold himself back, sensing her need to go slowly. To his surprise, when Max had called from the house to join them for a pre-dinner drink, it had been him who had ended the kiss, reluctantly, yes, but Sarah hadn't seemed to even hear Max.

There was a passion burning behind her grey eyes that hid so much. A passion at odds with the totally together, successful woman she was, in control of herself and her environment. But today, in his arms, even more than after the fundraising dinner, she'd let herself go.

Until he'd touched her shirt.

There was a story there. And where normally he was only interested in women who were after the same thing as him, with no complications, with Sarah he was surprising himself.

'Be a gentleman and put the kettle on again, honey,' Phoebe said to Max.

'I thought your claim is that firefighters aren't gentlemen and wouldn't know the first thing about chivalry if it hit them on the head?' countered Max as he stood and left for the kitchen.

'I would've thought firefighters and chivalry went hand in hand?' Sarah said as she caught Ned's eye and her hand fluttered to the neck of her shirt, the exact spot his hand had been when she'd pulled away from him so suddenly earlier. Was she thinking he'd been chivalrous then? Was chivalry equal to genuine concern? Because that's what had motivated his reaction.

'I think they might actually be mutually exclusive.' Phoebe laid down her knitting as she answered, her voice loud enough to carry to Max, who was clattering about in the kitchen. 'Max told me in our early stages that if he was with me but off duty when my toaster caught fire, he wouldn't come to my rescue except by dialling 000 for the fire department.' She cocked an eyebrow at her husband, who was returning with the laden teatray expertly balanced.

'Sarah, what say you? Any rebuttal for Phoebe's outrageous claim about firefighters?' Max asked.

Her gaze skittered straight to Ned and, far from looking away, she met it, held it and then grinned at him. 'I'll give the rights of rebuttal to Ned. What's your take on damsels in distress and white goods?' The reference to his white-goods comment when he'd shown her the fire station created a feeling of mutual understanding. It was a feeling he was liking more and more.

'For the record,' he said to the two women, 'if any electrical item, be it a kitchen appliance or otherwise, was ever to catch fire and I was there, I'd rescue you even if I was off duty.'

Phoebe looked at Sarah. 'Is that deserving of a revision of my theory? Shall I say most firefighters aren't chivalrous except a few rare gems?'

'Don't be too hasty, ladies,' chimed in Max.

'You have another explanation for Ned's offer?'

'Absolutely,' said Max, glancing from Ned to Sarah then back again before fixing Ned with a grin that made it clear what he was thinking. And leaving Ned wishing he could deck his mate. 'But I think I'd better keep it to myself.'

CHAPTER SIX

WHICH, reflected Sarah as she drove them both home half an hour later, had been a fitting place to end the evening, bringing them both straight back to where they'd begun the day: shadow-boxing around an acute awareness of their mutual attraction.

But, she suspected, where to Ned it simply held the promise of a fling, to her it meant much, much more. Physically baring herself came at a price. It went hand in hand with inviting rejection. It meant risking humiliation. It meant making herself vulnerable in a way she'd sworn she never would again.

It was all well and good when she wasn't in touching distance of Ned. As soon as she was, her logic turned to mush. The confined space of the car was positively zinging with the heat of unsatisfied desire and, from the way he was glancing at her every ten seconds or so before whipping his gaze away, he knew it as much as she did.

She pressed a single, shaking finger against her lips for a moment, recalling the delectable sensation of the bite of his teeth there just hours ago, before forcing herself to at least attempt a normal conversation. 'Thanks for today,' she said, rushing on when she realised he could interpret that in so many ways. 'Phoebe and Max are wonderful and it's so lovely they're expecting. I can't imagine how awful it must have been for her to lose her son.'

'She told you about Joe?'

'Yes.' From his surprise she gathered Phoebe didn't talk much about her little boy. 'She was showing me all the baby gear and said she knew she was overreacting but since she'd had a son and he'd died from a meningococcal infection, she couldn't help her anxiety.'

'Anxiety will be a major part of parenthood for her, but Max will support her through it. And I know we made a joke of it, but Max is convinced having every piece of child safety equipment will help her cope. I think he's afraid she won't set foot away from the baby otherwise.'

'I can only imagine how she must have felt. It would be the worst thing in the world, to bury your child.' Was it her imagination or did he stiffen with her words? She glanced his way once and then again. Something was amiss. 'What's wrong? What did I say?'

'I was just thinking about my mother. She lost both her husband and a son.'

'Your dad and your brother?'

He nodded. 'Dad died when I was little, as you know. It was a car accident. Danny was with him. He was killed too.'

'How awful for her, for both of you.'

'I try not to think about it too often. I was six, Danny was four, but I know it's still very much in Mum's mind.'

Despite having to find the right words to say to

families so often in the emergency department, words failed her now. Silence stretched between them as she tried to think of a response that wasn't gratuitous. She thought of how she would have felt if Tori had died all those years ago. They had really been just babies so she doubted it would have had the same impact on her. Ned had been six, so he'd have very clear memories of his little brother. Distracted by her musings, she indicated and changed lanes.

'Look out!' Ned shouted.

A motorbike had roared up in the inside lane at the same moment she'd crossed the painted lines. Yanking on the steering-wheel, she jerked the car back into the outside lane as the motorcyclist sped past.

Shaking, she slowed down, and would have stopped except that there was no place to do it. 'Sorry. He came out of nowhere.' There was a slight tremor in her voice, a strange mix between the fright she'd had and the desire which now seemed even more intensified.

'You OK?' He touched her on the shoulder, the feel of his hand electric even through the thickness of her fleecy top. 'Do you want me to drive?'

'I'm OK,' she said, and to prove it she indicated and pulled back into the lane after checking twice to make certain it was empty this time.

She was OK, or at least had been until he'd touched her. But OK didn't cover the burst of heat she'd just felt. She would've been more than OK if she could have stopped the car, hurled herself into his arms and, without hesitation, pursued this desire to its natural conclusion.

She'd seen desire flash in his eyes when he'd touched her: he wanted her. For tonight at least, if not beyond.

As for her, since that kiss this afternoon, it had no longer been a matter of whether to sleep with him.

Just when.

A shudder of anticipation mixed with fear ran through her as she admitted her decision to herself for the first time. If he rejected her, it was only going to have lasted a short time anyway. She'd had him pegged as a playboy in those early first meetings and now his best friends had confirmed he was not settling-down material.

With Alistair, she'd thought they'd been in a committed relationship, thought she'd meant something to him. More fool her. She knew better now. She wasn't going to give her heart away again. This would be a purely physical relationship, short and sweet. Where was the risk in that?

She knew where it was: the risk was Ned might take one look at the scar severing the valley between her breasts and call it a night. Or sleep with her and make himself scarce the first chance he got afterwards.

But if she went into this with her eyes wide open? If she was prepared to take that risk in order to indulge the incredible sensations that rushed through her at the mere thought of his hands on her body, then what could be the harm in throwing sensible behaviour out the window?

The freeway ended and Ned gave her directions to his mother's house. He'd told her he was house-sitting for her while she was away on a long-planned overseas trip, an arrangement that was suiting him, too. Since being promoted to head of CBR control he'd moved from the hills to the city and had been sharing a flat with another work colleague of questionable hygiene. He'd been happy, he'd said with a laugh, to escape and buy some time to find a more suitable arrangement.

Following his directions, she turned off the main road into a suburb she vaguely knew, and a few minutes later he indicated for her to turn into a driveway that led to a modern sandstone house with precise lines and shuttered windows.

Switching off the ignition, she glanced his way and her breath caught in her throat as they looked at each other. His eyes, an impossibly appealing green, were soft and warm with sleepiness and good wine, the reason she'd offered to drive. If he'd tensed when she'd asked about his dad, he wasn't showing it now.

'Not what you expected?'

'Not for you, no. I didn't realise I'd pictured it, and I know it doesn't belong to you, but it's definitely *not* the house I'd see as yours.'

'No?' The single word was heavy with invitation and flung her thoughts straight back into the ruby-red pool of desire that had been preoccupying her for the last ten minutes. 'Do tell.'

She hesitated, pretending to need time to think through her answer. Knowing where they'd been heading, part of her detailed imaginings had conjured up the house he'd belong in. She knew it all, down to the trees in the garden, but she spoke slowly, in a considered way, as if the blueprint wasn't already crystal-clear in her mind. Women about to embark on one-night flings shouldn't be imagining dream houses for their hopefully soon-to-be lover.

'A rambling bungalow,' she said, 'with a verandah wrapped right round. Your favourite spot would be slouching on the front steps.' She was babbling but, as she talked, she knew it was exactly the sort of place she'd conjure up for him. But it wasn't complete yet. 'A great big black dog would be draped over your knees while you bury your fingers behind his ears and rub him in the exact way that never fails to make him floppy.'

The tremor in her voice told both of them she had absolute belief in his power to make any creature go floppy with satisfaction. It was the dog she was talking about, she reminded herself as she removed the keys from the ignition and Ned opened the car door, fixing her with an amused smile that she could see all too well as the internal light came on. The light bathed both their faces in yellow, spotlighting the double entendres zipping about them. He eased himself from the passenger seat, closed the door and came around to open hers, giving her a few seconds to regain her composure and admonish herself against making any more revealing slips about just how readily she could conjure up images of him.

'You know one thing you got right…' His voice was gravelly, his green eyes still amused as he opened her door and reached for her arm, helping her from the car.

As they stood, chest to chest, close enough for their breath to mingle, she aimed for composed but fell shockingly short and whispered, 'What?'

'I have,' he said as he bent his head closer to hers until his mouth was a mere inch from her ear, 'a knack for always knowing the right way to rub. Every time. In every circumstance.'

'Every time?' Her question came out on a jittery tremor as he fixed her with a look, making his meaning plain. There were no double entendres now. It was all in the open, all on the table and all up to her. Back out and head for home or make her fantasies pale into insignificance against what Ned was offering: a night in his arms, under his spell. Nothing stood in their way except her; equally true, there was nothing to expect afterwards except an ending, with or without a blatant rejection of her flaws.

'Would you like to come inside?'

The perfect fling was being offered to her like a juicy, crimson plum, hers for the plucking.

She looked into his eyes, took a deep breath and lost herself in his delicious scent, the scent of berries and warm earth, remnants of a day spent in the sun with friends replacing the woodsy scent she'd come to associate with him.

What was she was seconds away from consenting to?

It would be as simple as nodding yes, as natural as moving an infinitesimal degree closer to the warmth of his body in the night air.

She did both. Then there was no hesitation, no room for questions or doubts. This was where she needed to be, where she was meant to be, and even when he'd ushered her inside and they were standing in the doorway of a bedroom she was conscious of nothing but an urgent need to be with him.

'Sarah.' Her name was a caress on his lips. He hadn't kissed her yet, he'd simply led her here, and she knew he'd given her that time deliberately. Had given her time to make sure she had no doubts. For once she didn't need the time. For once nothing mattered except here and now. Today's kisses in the barn had led them to this point—there was nowhere else she could go and still stay sane. 'Are you sure?'

'Yes.' A tremor ran the length of her as she raised her eyes to meet his, filled with his desire for her. His gaze dropped to her lips and she could feel it almost physically. He raised a hand to touch her lower lip between his fingers, just as he'd done with his teeth and mouth that afternoon, his thumb trailing little circles on her cheek.

'You are so beautiful.' Her heart stopped at his words then started racing with a helter-skelter crazy beat as his voice caught on a rasp. She knew then that he was as affected as she was and she could let herself believe that he was suffering just as much as she was from wanting him. He moved his thumb in a tiny movement at her temple and she all but passed out as her eyelids fluttered closed and she drifted off into the sensation of pure bliss, unable to think of anything beyond the fact he was making her melt, her limbs now liquid.

'You were right.' The words came out on a whisper, the most she was capable of. 'You know exactly how to rub.' And at that, her knees went shaky, just as they had in the barn. Again, he caught her and lifted her into his arms as though she was weightless. Held firmly against his chest, her head nestled against his shoulder, she allowed herself to breathe deeply, lost in a sense of awareness and anticipation. She closed her eyes again as his scent surrounded her, cushioning her. She could picture the waves of desire that surrounded them, wrapping her in a kaleidoscope of virtual colour.

She felt him nudge the door open with his foot and knew he was carrying her to his bed, his step steady and oh, so certain. Conscious thought returned for long enough to make her tense briefly, waiting for her recurring anxiety to surface, but it was as though she were watching herself on screen, a scene she'd seen time and again, but this time the next part of the scene was unfamiliar. The anxiety didn't come, the nerves and the fear simply weren't there. In Ned's arms, all she felt was safe. Beautiful. Desirable.

He lowered her to the bed, sliding a pillow beneath her head with infinite care. She opened her eyes and blinked in the darkness to find him. He eased himself above her, supported by his arms, and she reached up and circled his biceps with her hands, marvelling at how, with his muscles rippling as he supported his weight, she could scarcely stretch her thumbs to meet her fingers. His breath was coming fast, its warmth on her face, and they stayed like that, poised to move this attraction between them on, but he was in no hurry. As his hot, intense and dark gaze moved over her breasts, rising and falling beneath her shirt, she tensed very slightly but the feeling passed into nothingness as she relaxed to her very bones beneath his look of desire.

The waiting was agony but it was also exquisite, the delicious sense of anticipation doing battle with her competing need to pull him down to her and demand him *now*.

'Ned.' She whispered his name, and he groaned and bent his head to hers, lowering his body until it covered the length of her. She wanted to feel his weight on her, needed to wring every last sensation that this was real and happening to *her*. She felt his lips roving over her neck, pausing there as if waiting for her reaction, but she had none except to urge him on, lower, to do everything to her, all the many things she'd dreamt about this last week. Had it only been for one week she'd known the magic his mouth could work?

As he moved to nibble on her earlobe, his hands traced a line from button to button on her shirt, teasing, teasing, until finally she could wait no longer and she guided his fingers to the top button, showing him what she wanted. In seconds, her buttons were undone, and ever so gently he parted the fabric of her shirt, running his fingers with the lightest touch over her breast—the lightest touch but it was a touch that seemed to be a direct stairway to nirvana and once more she felt herself melting. While his teeth teased her earlobe, his fingers were working their way in ever smaller circles over the warm skin of her breast. He was moving achingly slowly so that when he finally touched her nipple, she was so primed for it, so tight with expectation, she leapt slightly in his arms.

'Are you OK?' He moved his mouth from her earlobe to rasp his question.

'Don't stop' was all she could say. Two such simple little words but ones she hadn't said in a long, long time.

And it seemed it was the last reassurance they'd both been waiting for, for now his mouth was on hers, and he was kissing her like she was the answer to his prayers. He rolled partly off her and when it seemed he was about to move, she pulled him down to her by the hair on the back of his head, needing that kiss to go on for ever. But she hadn't needed to worry; he wasn't done yet. She relaxed as his hand found the globe of her breast again and resumed his lazy rubbing of her nipple

Take a look at what's on offer at

www.millsandboon.co.uk

between his fingers. Her head fell back deeper onto the pillow as the exquisite attention he was giving her threatened to tip her over the edge.

Then suddenly her lips were cold and she cried out as she realised he'd stopped kissing her. Her protest was cut short as she felt the heat of his tongue lap her nipple, then his other hand moved decisively across the mound of her breast, and over the dip of her cleavage. She held her breath, freezing for a second as his fingers found the raised ridge of skin that marred her breastbone, dividing one breast from the other. She waited for him to hesitate, to raise his mouth to ask her what it was, why it was, what was wrong with her. But the questions didn't come and the hesitation didn't come. His fingers instead ran along the length of the scar tissue with a touch so utterly sweet a lump caught in her throat. And then when he reached the end of the line of scar tissue he simply ran his fingers back up again, until his hand was poised beneath her other breast, and then cupping it, he began tormenting her again with a sweet caress.

There had been no discernible moment of shock. And the realisation it wasn't going to happen was exactly what she needed to immerse herself in the pleasures of Ned's love-making. It was exactly what she needed to allow herself to let go in a way she'd never imagined possible until Ned had entered her life and her dreams. Now she was in his arms and in his bed. In the almost total darkness of the room he'd freed her to give herself up to being the object of his glorious attentions.

Sunlight was peeking through the curtains as Sarah stretched her arms above her head, enjoying the sensation of lazing in a man's bed. 'Perfect' didn't come close to describing the heaven of spending a night in the arms of Ned Kellaway. 'Perfect' didn't come close to describing a morning in his arms either.

In the wee small hours of the new day she'd woken to find her body already responding to him as he'd stroked her thigh and then extended his touch to stroke over her belly, then higher, onto the rounded swells of her breasts, before she'd murmured something like 'More' and had pulled him down to her…

Afterwards, she'd slipped back into the gorgeous slumber of the deeply satisfied and had woken only a few moments ago, with a grin fit to reflect the incredible memories of the night, but alone in the rumpled sheets of the bed. She could smell coffee brewing and could hear the shower running somewhere in the house.

She was reluctant to get up. But if she didn't get up, she'd run the risk of having to get dressed in front of him. The ease she'd felt under his gaze and caresses last night had been nothing short of a miracle. But hoping she'd suddenly overcome her anxieties after just one night and could start parading about naked was ludicrous.

Being naked in full daylight, her imperfections revealed in the morning sun, was one step she was quite, quite sure she'd couldn't take. In the cold hard light of day, would Ned react differently? He'd seen her now, and although he hadn't reacted with shock or revulsion as his fingers had felt her scar for the first time, he must at least now have questions about how it had got there.

She felt like she was in the dock, waiting for her sentence to be handed down.

The hallway creaked with a footfall and it was only then Sarah realised the shower had long since stopped running and Ned was on his way back to his room— and she was still naked. Scanning the floor, she spotted her clothes on the other side of the room.

The door was opening and there was no time to make a dash for her top but there was an old T-shirt of Ned's on the bed. Grabbing it, she yanked it over her head, pulling it down roughly by the hem just as the door opened and Ned came in backwards, carrying something. He'd bumped the door open with his backside so that all she saw at first was the damp expanse of a perfect, tanned naked back, covered from the waist down by a fluffy white towel.

Turning, his grin on seeing her awake was instant.

'Good morning, sleepyhead,' he said as he nodded towards the tray he'd laid out with huge round cups of steaming coffee and hot buttered toast. 'I brought refreshments.'

She barely glanced at the tray she was so enamoured by the vision he presented in daylight. Perfection from head to toe, and she knew from first-hand experience that beneath the towel the theme of perfection continued unabated.

He took her breath away and she could only think, This is it, I've died and gone to heaven. A heaven where men were tall and strong, had not an ounce of spare flesh, and had unblemished skin that stretched tightly over muscle and sinew. His muscles flexed as he laid the tray down on the table next to his side of the bed. Stepping away, he grabbed a pair of boxer shorts from a chest of drawers, then, still with his back to her, dropped his towel, giving her a glimpse of yet more perfection. He had a backside so gorgeous it was all she could do not to launch herself over the covers and sink her teeth into its flesh. Sitting down on the bed, apparently unaware the mere sight of him was enough to send her over the edge, he slid first one leg then the other into the shorts, then stood to ease them up until he was covered and she found herself able to breathe normally again.

Now he lay back on the bed and rolled onto his side, until he was resting on one elbow. His grin was so full of mischief and satisfaction she again felt the flames fan the glow of hope that had burned so bright in her last night. With his brown hair tousled and damp he resembled nothing so much as an adorable, life-loving, warm, fluffy, playful puppy.

And then the next moment these thoughts were banished as he muttered, 'Come here, you,' and tugged on the hem of the T-shirt, his T-shirt, pulling her down to him from where she still sat, hugging her knees. She knew her lips had parted the moment he'd reached out for her. Her body was responding now on its own, separate to any conscious input from her. One gesture and she was ready for him, wanting him, wanting last night to happen again, and again.

She eased down to him, her face above his now, and there they stayed, his pupils enlarging with each passing second their gazes held, desire deepening the colour of his irises. He was breathing just a touch faster whereas she was holding her breath. He raised his head and caught her earlobe in his teeth again, and automatically she closed her eyes, the better to immerse herself in the sensations rippling straight down an inbuilt pathway she hadn't known existed, straight from her ear to her belly. His hand slid beneath the T-shirt, stroking her waist, his touch rhythmic. When he eased the hem of the shirt higher, the sense of being somewhere else, out of herself, evaporated. The room was light and the sun rippled through the slats of the wooden shutters, casting fingers of light that fell across the bed like arrows pointing her out. The T-shirt provided only the simplest of protection and as he eased the fabric higher and his fingers moved over her belly towards her breasts, she pulled away.

He stopped immediately, which she'd known he would. She'd been right, she thought incongruously, to say firefighters were chivalrous. This one was, anyway, there was no doubting that, and it made her wish all the harder this could be different, that she could be different.

'I know it looks good on you,' he said, as she tugged the T-shirt back down over her waist, 'but I was kinda hoping we could lose it for a while.' His smile was gentle, kind, and she knew instinctively *he* recognised her self-consciousness and was making light of the situation. For her. 'At least while our coffee cools down.'

She ran a hand through her hair and sat up, trying to find the words to explain herself. Words that didn't make her sound like the uptight girl he must think her. But there weren't any because, deep down, she knew she *was* uptight, at least where this was concerned. Tori didn't have this problem, Tori was quite comfortable bouncing about with plunging necklines displaying half her scar in one go. Why couldn't they be more alike?

'I know you have a scar and I know you're self-conscious about it, but you don't need to be, you know,' he said conversationally as he sat up, plumped up the pillows behind them and then eased her back until she was resting against the bedhead. 'There's not a spot on your body I'm not ready and willing to kiss any time you give the word.' He settled himself next to her so they weren't looking at each other, and she marvelled that they were here propped up in bed like a real couple, chatting so easily about something that went straight to the core of her. He reached out to pick her hand up in his and pressed his lips against the soft skin of her palm as if to underline his point about kissing. 'And there's not a single bit of you I don't consider utterly gorgeous.' He turned her hand over and kissed the back of it, and she looked down on the top of his ruffled head with wonder. 'Even without my shirt.'

'Are you sure?'

'Positive. Why would a scar make any difference? I've got plenty, you're welcome to count them all if you like.' His grin was cheeky, his dimple flashing in and out. 'You don't look convinced.'

'I'm just so used to my scar being an issue.'

'What do you mean?'

'My ex-boyfriend would never touch it. He almost made a point of avoiding it. He liked everything in his world perfect. He made it clear I was not.'

'He told you that?'

'Pretty much.' More like, every chance he got, as explicitly as he could.

'I hope you dumped him quickly.'

'Actually, in the end, he left me for someone else, telling me it was my fault because I was flawed.' She shrugged, embarrassed to admit how gullible she'd been, to allow Alistair to undermine her confidence so badly.

Ned was quiet for a moment. The part of Sarah that was still so ready to doubt herself wondered if he had been turned off her just by her admission of what she knew had been weakness. 'I'm glad he's out of your life. It leaves room for me.' His voice was low and warm. 'Come here and I'll show you again just how perfect you are.'

He pulled her into his arms, sliding his hands under the T-shirt as he kissed her, leaving her head spinning. He hadn't rejected her, he'd called her perfect. She kissed him back while her body melted beneath his touch. Thoughts twirled in her mind until, out of the kaleidoscope of images and words, one truth emerged and flashed behind her closed lids: she was in serious danger of falling in love with this gorgeous, thought-ful, daredevil of a sweet-talking firefighter.

And although she was still scared, although it had been years since a man had seen her naked, the shock of her realisation was enough to jolt her into action as the pieces of the puzzle fell into place. He hadn't rejected her and from the way he was talking, would it be so very foolish to start hoping this might be more than a one-night stand?

It had been the single most defining sexual experience of his life. The fact that work commitments for them both meant he wouldn't see her again until tonight, more than forty-eight hours after they'd parted, had come close to doing his head in.

He was attempting to sort through a pile of mail but

even that menial task was proving difficult as his thoughts kept returning to memories of Saturday night. And Sunday morning. All the way up to Sunday lunchtime when Sarah had left for work.

He picked up some of his mum's mail as she'd asked him to email her anything that looked important. He'd thought it strange at the time, but as he turned a heavy cream envelope in his hands a trickle of unease ran down his spine. He slid a finger under the flap of the envelope, pulling out a single sheet of paper. The letter was from the organ donation foundation. He read the words three times.

Surely his mum hadn't done what this letter stated?

But it seemed she must have, since the third read-through told him exactly the same thing: his mother had placed a direction on his brother's file agreeing to contact should any of Daniel's transplant recipients seek it.

Apparently that had now happened.

The letter went on to say that should the Kellaway family still agree to contact, would a family member please contact the office for the recipient's contact details.

He thrust his chair backwards, hard, not caring in the slightest when it skidded across the tiled floor and hit the filing cabinet behind him with a resounding thwack.

What sort of a damn fool idea was this?

He knew his mum had consented to organ donation for both his dad and his little brother. He knew it, and he also knew there was no point thinking about that. What's done was done and while it was a good thing in the abstract, who the hell needed the specifics?

'And,' he said, stalking to the window and staring unseeingly out at the city street shimmering in the heat of the summer below, 'that's the end of it!'

He rolled the letter up and stood hitting it against the palm of his other hand, thwack, thwack, thwack, as if by hitting it, the content might be encouraged to redraft itself or, better still, disappear.

His email notifier did its job and announced he had new mail.

It was enough to snap him out of the void he'd just been in. Enough to get him to place the letter on his scanner and send the document as an email attachment to his mum, as she'd requested. There was no way of knowing when she'd next pick up her emails. But he was damn sure he didn't want the letter on his mind. He clicked send and watched the mail fold itself up and vanish.

If only he could have done that with the letter in the first place.

Who needed to go back and mess with what was perfectly well settled and better left alone?

He continued to pace around the room until his phone rang, interrupting his steps. He snatched it up from its cradle.

'Ned?'

His mum. 'Hi, Mum, how's the cruise?'

'Brilliant. Auntie Barb and I just can't believe we didn't do this years ago. But I'll fill you in when I get home. I just wanted to speak to you about the letter you just emailed me. Do you think you could contact the foundation and get the recipient's details for me?'

'I can but what's the hurry? You've only had the letter for five minutes. Surely it can wait till you get home.'

'I know, but I've been thinking about this moment

for years. I've always wondered whether I did the right thing, donating your dad's and Danny's organs. I know objectively I did, but from where I stand as a mother and a wife, was it the right thing to do?' In the background, he could hear the dim roar of traffic, the sounds of a city somewhere on the other side of the world. Somewhere he'd prefer to be right now instead of having to deal with this. 'Did it change lives? Do people who got a second chance know how lucky they are?'

'I don't get it, Mum. It's done. You can assume it's a good thing you did. Why do you need the details?'

'You're asking me for a rational explanation for something I feel emotionally. But if a word will help you understand, then "closure" is probably about the best I can do.'

'You don't have closure?'

'Not really. And now there's someone who wants to thank us, someone whose mother got to keep their child, someone whose life might make the tiniest bit more sense of our loss of Danny and your dad. Hang on a sec.' Her voice went muffled for a moment and he imagined her holding the receiver to her chest as she spoke to someone. An image came to him of him as a little boy interrupting her phone call. She'd placed her hand on the receiver and asked him patiently, kindly to wait. Endlessly patient. Patient and understanding. He wasn't showing her any of that in return. Was it so much for her to ask? Opening up the past so she could lay her youngest son and husband to rest a little more peacefully? He sat down, waiting for her to come back on the line.

'Sorry, sweetheart, Auntie Barb is just ordering room service for us.'

'OK, Mum, I'll do it today. The details will be waiting for you when you get home.'

'Thanks. And, Ned? You might not need the closure like I do, but it also might not be the dreaded experience you're anticipating.'

She rang off. Swinging in his chair, he stretched to the corner of his desk to retrieve the letter. This was probably best done in the same way as removing a sticky plaster: quickly, to get the pain over and done with.

Dialling the number written in bold on the letter, he didn't even have time to hope for a recorded message before a high-pitched voice welcomed him to the organ donor foundation, told him she was Mandy and asked how she could help.

Draft him another letter, telling him the first was a mistake?

Instead, he told Mandy what she could do for him. Mandy went through some identifying information protocol in a scarily upbeat way, telling him between his answers it was only her second day there, she was a temp and the file manager was at a meeting. But he could imagine the white-toothed smile flashing. Not to worry, she'd seen the file match system work at least three times and it was easy-peasy-lemon-squeezy.

She talked him through each step of the process as she entered Danny's details into the computer to find the recipient match.

'Oh, here we go! Got it, first time and all!'

If she was waiting for congratulations from him, she'd better be a patient temp, he thought. Luckily she announced if he'd just wait a jiffy, she'd scoot right over and pull the match to his brother's file right this minute, and give him the contact details.

He'd never have thought there could be a receptionist who could make finding out who was walking about with his dead brother's organs stitched inside them a warm and fuzzy experience. But it seemed it was his lucky day and Mandy was doing her level best to turn organ donation into the most fun he'd ever had.

He lowered his head into his hands and sat there groaning softly as he heard someone he presumed was Mandy humming loudly in the background.

'You there?' His head jerked up as Mandy's shrill tone pierced his eardrums. Where else would he be? He thought of Sarah and the soft, modulated tones of her voice and felt a physical ache to see her again.

'Got a pen?'

He sighed a 'yes' and got ready to write.

'This must be a really exciting time, finding out whose life your brother saved.' Ned felt his jaw drop at the stupidity of the assumption and deemed it not worth acknowledging. 'Now, the phone number is…' She reeled off a string of digits and he dutifully recorded them. 'And the surname is R-I-C-H-A-R-D-S-O-N and the first name is…' She stated the name then spelt it out for good measure.

'I beg your pardon?'

She repeated the information and he muttered something like thanks and hung up while she was still wishing him the happiest day.

Not an experience to dread?

'Bloody hell, Mum.' He tore the piece of paper off the pad and held it up to the light.

Sarah Richardson.

He dug out his mobile and hit the search function.

The numbers matched.

Just as he'd known they would. The moment Mandy had answered the phone, he should've known fate had decided today was a good day for kicking Ned Kellaway where no man should ever be kicked.

'And that's what comes of digging around in the past where no one in their right mind would ever go.'

He grabbed his wallet, sunglasses and mobile and punched in a message before quickly hitting 'send'.

This was a set of cards he only knew how to deal with one way: a minimum of twenty laps of the Olympic pool with no need to talk to anyone else. The pool was his haven and the place where he did his best thinking. Women might laugh at men for going into their caves when the going got tough but there was something to be said for being able to put everything else aside as you focused on a single, important issue. 'Laugh away, world,' he muttered, as he shoved open the door. 'Laugh away, 'cos this black bear's heading into his cave and rolling a bloody great boulder in front of the entrance for good measure.'

CHAPTER SEVEN

SARAH heard the front door slam and quickly tried to look busy, knowing she needed to avoid meeting her twin's eyes if she was going to have any chance of pretending everything was OK. She ducked into the bathroom and started removing her make-up as Tori walked into the kitchen, tossing the mail onto the table with a thud.

'I didn't expect you to be here, I thought you had a hot date.' Tori started sorting through the mail, putting it into various piles.

Sarah breathed a sigh of relief that her sister wasn't looking at her. 'So did I, but he's just cancelled.'

'What happened?'

'He didn't say, he just sent a text message. I tried calling, but his phone is switched off.'

'Put the news on. He's probably busy with some emergency. I'm sure he'll get back to you when he can.'

Tori immediately had a perfectly reasonable explanation, one that didn't involve her second-guessing herself, whereas she had automatically assumed the cancellation had somehow been her fault. She rinsed her face as she tested Tori's theory. It was viable.

Tori was tearing open a letter. 'There's a letter here from the organ donor foundation, addressed to me. You haven't heard anything yet, have you?'

Sarah shook her head. 'What does it say?' She watched Tori's face as she read her letter, saw her sister's broad grin and knew Tori had the response she'd been hoping for.

'The foundation has my donor family on file consenting to contact. They've passed on my request and if they are still agreeable the family will contact the foundation and will be given my details. Fingers crossed, I may be able to thank them after all!'

'That's fantastic, I really hope it all works out.'

'I hope you hear something soon, too. That really would be perfect.'

Would it? She wasn't so certain but she was leaving it up to fate to decide.

Did the same apply to a relationship with Ned? Was everything out of her control? Unless he answered his phone there probably wasn't much she could do. So for tonight, at least, she'd go with Tori's hypothesis and believe the cancelled date had been nothing to do with her.

Sarah scooted from the patient she'd just finished with in search of the triage nurse. She was working on the basis of taking anything and everything that would keep her mind off Ned. It had been forty hours now with no word from him. It was getting harder to stick with Tori's theory. There was no emergency that would stop Ned from contacting her for that long if he'd wanted to.

With each passing minute it was getting harder to remember he'd called her perfect and easier to recall he only ever had short-term relationships. She'd jumped into bed with him with her eyes wide open so she only had herself to blame.

At least it was busy today, so she didn't have to scrounge for work. 'Sarah,' the triage nurse said and immediately Sarah arrived by her side, 'can you take the patient in cubicle three?'

'What have we got?'

'A rookie firefighter who collapsed during training.'

When had she ever treated so many firemen? She knew it was probably just her increased awareness since meeting Ned and taking on the CBR work. A rookie she could deal with.

She pulled back the curtain and caught her breath. Standing next to the man lying in the bed was Ned.

He looked up as she entered and although he smiled, she knew immediately it was strained, and hardly full of pleasure at seeing her. And yet one look at him and she knew then and there that if he gave her even the simplest of reasons for not calling, she'd jump back into bed with him the first chance she got.

There was no denying it, her reaction was so immediate, intense and physical it stunned her. Her heart rate soaring, her knees going weak. There was no doubt about it, her resolve to play things cool, calm and collected was outmatched by her libido.

Somehow she managed to get her professional persona back in place, acknowledging Ned with a 'Hello' and a smile. Then she turned straight to the man on the bed and picked up the chart.

'Ryan, I'm Dr Sarah Richardson. Can you tell me what happened?'

'I just got a bit dizzy while we were doing a training exercise.'

'What exactly were you doing?'

'A stair climb,' said Ned, meaning she now had to look at him and risk her knees going wobbly again. 'Remember the big tower you saw at the station?' She nodded. As long as she didn't have to get her powers of speech working while she looked at him, she'd be fine. 'They have to run up to the top in full gear, with BA cylinders. The temperature would be around fifty degrees, replicating scenarios they'd come across on the job. Ryan collapsed a couple of flights from the top, complaining of dizziness, and he couldn't stand any light.'

Another nod before she turned with relief back to Ryan to check the monitors the nurse had attached, her powers of speech returning once she refocused on her patient. 'Any other symptoms? Headaches? Nausea?'

'A bit of a headache but I'm not dizzy now.'

'Your blood pressure is low and your pulse is slow. We'll do an ECG to check your heart but I suspect you've had a vasovagal attack.'

'A what?'

'A vasovagal attack. It's a fancy term for fainting. Probably caused by dehydration.'

'So I'm fine? I can go?'

'Not yet. You need to be rehydrated so it doesn't happen again. I want to do the ECG and run a couple of litres of fluid into you and then we'll see.' She turned to Ned. 'Could I have a word?' There, she'd managed to sound professional, calm and in control. Although managing to string five words together hardly meant she was out of the woods. There was still every chance she'd reveal the emotional roller-coaster ride she'd been on since Sunday.

Ned followed her out of the cubicle as the nurse set up a drip for Ryan and Sarah led him to the doctors' lounge, checking the room was empty before entering.

'What's wrong with Ryan? Do I need to call his family?' Ned asked as soon as the door closed behind them. Her hopes that he'd launch straight into a personal discussion evaporated. Of course he'd assume she'd brought him here to discuss a medical issue, but it wasn't what she was after.

'Ryan's fine, I would have told him if I thought things were more serious. I wanted to talk to you.' She hesitated, unsure now about the wisdom of trying to have this discussion at work. Or at all. What if he was standing there wishing she'd just go away, and she was about to get personal? Still, she'd started this now and at the end of the day, she needed to know. 'Did you get my message on Tuesday night?'

'Yes.'

She hesitated. Why did he have to have it dragged out of him? 'Is everything OK? We were going out to dinner…' She let her words trail off. Needing to know was one thing but begging for attention? She wouldn't go there.

'It's not a good time for me right now, Sarah.' He ran a finger around the neck of his T-shirt and although he looked her in the eye, he only held her gaze for the briefest moment before glancing elsewhere.

What the hell did that mean? 'Not a good time to have this discussion or not a good time for dating?'

'There are a few things I need to sort out.'

'Ned, please, just tell me what the problem is.' She refrained from expressing her frustration with a good, hard stamp of her foot. Just.

'It involves you and your heart transplant.'

'What?' She sat down on the nearest chair as he said the words she'd known all along just had to come between them.

Had he fooled her so well she'd imagined he'd accepted her, and her scar, but really he was just like Alistair? She wasn't perfect so he wasn't interested any more? He'd got what he wanted, another notch on his bedpost, and now he was gone.

'You wrote to the foundation. You wanted to find your donor family.'

Sarah nodded. 'Who told you that?'

'The foundation. There's no easy way to tell you this.' His gaze met hers again, then slid away as he went on, 'You have my brother's heart. Danny was your donor.'

'What? This is a joke, right?' Or a bad dream. What had she missed? Where had Ned got his information? 'How do you know that?'

'Mum had notified the foundation she was interested in meeting with Danny's recipient so they contacted her when they got your letter. Mum asked me to ring them to get the recipient's details. It's you.'

'What does that mean?' Any moment, he'd say, 'Gotcha!' Wouldn't he? Or she'd wake up. This just couldn't be happening.

'I don't know what it means. I need time to work out how I feel. It completely changes you and me, I can't pretend it doesn't. It's just too weird.'

He means I'm weird. Her libido disappeared under a blanket of disappointment and despair.

She looked up at Ned, hoping for some sign he hadn't really given up on them, for some small consolation, but he was keeping his face averted. Eye contact was not what he was after.

She knew the drill for a man not wanting her. She struggled to her feet, fighting to reassemble her dignity. 'I'd better check on Ryan. I'll tell him you'll be in the waiting area.' She had to get out of there. There was no way she was going to give him the satisfaction of seeing her cry.

Hot-footing it down the corridor and straight into the closest restroom, all she could think as she gripped the basin and looked at her wild eyes in the mirror was what did this mean? And she had no answers. She'd always felt her heart belonged to her. She knew it hadn't started off that way and the medication she took was a daily reminder, but to all intents and purposes it was her heart beating in her chest.

She knew it set her apart from others, that there were some who'd never quite be able to deal with the thought that her heart had come from someone who had died.

She'd hoped Ned was different.

But it seemed she was mistaken.

The rest of the thirteen women gathered for Tori's girls' night were living it up and Sarah was struggling to match their pace. She'd never felt less like celebrating.

She was attempting to at least look as though she was enjoying herself but she didn't think she was fooling Tori.

They'd finished dinner and were now off to check out the latest city pub to receive an expensive make-over.

It seemed as though the traditional pub was going the way of the dinosaurs.

Pushing open the heavy, modern wooden and steel doors, Sarah was surprised they'd been allowed in—the pub was bursting at the seams.

'Look at all the men!' said Hattie. Sarah wondered if she'd rub her hands together to underline the glee in her voice.

'I *love* Friday nights in the city,' added Georgie, similarly gleeful. 'Let's get 'em, girls!' And Sarah refrained from cringing as Georgie did, in fact, rub her hands together.

Tonight every conversation had been men, men, men and it was men as far as the eye could see, too. Which was fine under ordinary circumstances, Sarah was more than happy in male company. But not now, not when she'd so recently been ceremoniously, well, ditched, for want of a better word.

Men!

Pushing their way through the crowd to the back of the room, they found the girls ahead had already, by some small miracle, secured a table and sent a posse up to the bar for drinks. Champagne all round. Five of the women had already peeled off into the crowd in search of men, known or unknown.

Those nominated to fetch drinks returned to the table and handed out champagne, then the toasts started again. 'Here's to weddings, yours most specifically!'

'Here's to finding myself a man before I'm over the hill.'

'And to the one I *have* found getting around to proposing before I'm over the hill.'

Since the average age of the women was somewhere around twenty-six, the toasts weren't intended to be taken seriously. At least, Sarah hoped not.

Hattie slid into the last seat at the table, glowing, which was a give-away for the subject of her breathless announcement. 'Georgie's scored!'

'She's only been here ten minutes. Has she *scored* scored or is she just on the way?'

'Scored as in has the cutest guy hanging on her every word. I'm going back. He has friends!' Hattie clapped her hands together as ten female heads craned at varying angles of discomfort and with no regard for circumspection to try and spot Georgie. The questions and squeals buzzed over the table.

'Where is she?'

'Ooh, I can see her!'

'But I can't see him, he's got his back to us.'

'What's he wearing? Is that a uniform?'

Sarah couldn't help herself. At the mention of a uniform she was turning in her seat like the rest of the girls.

One quick glance was all she needed. All she saw was a broad back in a navy blue T-shirt with 'MFS' stencilled across it, but it was him, definitely him. Luckily she was sitting or her knees would definitely have let her down this time. As it was, the few sips of champagne she'd had churned unpleasantly in her stomach and the room spun.

She blinked to clear her vision, just to make sure, but there was no doubting it. Even his back was distinctive, the way he sat easy in his skin, relaxed at the bar but not slouching, a drink in one hand, resting it on the bar, while Georgie, just visible around the side of his large frame, carried on an animated conversation. Since he wasn't looking in another direction, she could only assume that Hattie was right and Ned was, in fact, hanging on Georgie's every word.

Again she blinked, trying to clear the picture of Ned with the impossibly pretty Georgie gazing adoringly up at him, her face alight with pleasure.

No use, the picture stuck. If anything, it was clearer now. She'd been a short-term fling, in apparently trademark-Ned style. Whether he'd ended it because that was his habit and her transplant was a convenient excuse or whether it was solely because of her operation was irrelevant now. It was over and, apparently, he was straight back on the singles scene while she nursed a broken heart. It was ludicrous to think she'd meant enough to him that he'd miss even a night at the pub because of her. For what?

She stiffened as she felt a blush creep over her cheeks and Tori must have noticed her reaction.

'Is that him?' Tori mouthed across the table. Sarah gave the tiniest nod of her head. 'Are you OK?'

Sarah shrugged in answer to her sister. Was she OK? If she wasn't, it was only a bruised ego causing it. That would right itself in time. She hoped.

As Hattie left the table a few of the others called out requests to let them know if the good-looking guy had any more friends, especially if the back of them looked as good as the one Georgie had found.

'I feel increasingly lucky I'm already married,' said Annie, a work friend of Tori's, in an aside to Sarah, as talk at the table turned back to men in general. A little older than Sarah and Tori, she was the only one of Tori's friends who had already settled down. 'What about you? You don't seem as giddy over the prospects of the men here tonight as most of the girls. Are you settled down or just older and wiser?'

'No to the first, yes to the second but I'm not any wiser.' She may not be giddy either but she'd fallen hard. Hard and fast with little reason to believe it would be reciprocated. So maybe that was giddiness. It definitely wasn't wisdom.

Tori came around behind Sarah and slung her arms about her sister's neck. 'Sorry, Annie, I have to borrow my sister for a minute.'

She pulled Sarah away from the table over to the far end of the bar where she squeezed her way into a spot that didn't really exist, between two groups of rowdy people. 'Relax, he can't see you here, there're too many people. Are you OK?'

'I'll live.' She shrugged, knowing she was convincing neither of them. She was still licking her wounds, still trying to work out how she felt about her donor news, hoping, really, that the issue would go away, that he'd change his mind that it mattered. And hoping he'd change his mind about her. 'I'm embarrassed, that's all.'

'He doesn't look like he's unreasonable. Cute, hot? Yes. Unreasonable?' Tori shook her head in answer to her own question. 'Don't give up so easily. If you fell for him, I'd guess there's something real there so don't go giving up at the first sniff of rejection.'

'It was hardly a sniff, Tori, he was pretty direct about it. Blunt, even.'

Tori shrugged. 'So? People change their minds.

Maybe he'll realise it doesn't matter, that you matter more.'

'Maybe, maybe not. I'll get over it.' Seeing Tori wasn't buying her pitch, she added, 'I'm just embarrassed he's moved on so quickly, that's all.'

'My foot, that's all. You went rigid when you saw him and then you sighed. With regret.'

'I don't sigh. Not over men, anyway.'

'Yes, you do, and you cry, too.' Tori made a show of checking her sister's eyes for tears. 'You sit there with your book and pretend not to watch those romantic comedy movies when I am, but if I pause it for any reason I know you're twitching for me to get back. And at the happy-ever-after endings, you always make an excuse to leave the room and then I hear you shuffling about in the kitchen to get a tissue.' Tori had her hands on her hips, warming to her theme. Since she was the most tenacious person Sarah knew, she also knew she wouldn't let it drop until she had the admission she was looking for. 'You haven't fooled me, no matter what you like to pretend to yourself. You're as much a sucker for a happy-ever-after as the next woman.'

Sarah glanced over in Ned's direction and found that, despite Tori's claims to the contrary, she could now see him better than before. As the bar was in an 'L' shape, and they were on different sides, Ned was now in profile. He was also making a fair fist of looking as though he was enjoying himself.

He'd looked like that with her.

But he'd replaced her quickly enough.

She didn't suppose it much mattered who he was with. Ned liked women. Unfortunately, he liked them far too much to want to be with just one. One at a time, maybe, but not one for all time.

And seeing him now was far too harsh a reminder that somewhere deep down inside her, she'd been building castles in the clouds. A little part of her had been dreaming ridiculous dreams of a future together. She bit her lip and, too late, remembered she was under scrutiny.

'Would it be so awful to take a risk and go over there? What's the worst that can happen?'

'Rejection.'

'Not all men are like Alistair, my Harry's proof of that. What if Ned is your Harry? You can't leave him to women like Georgie. It's time you forgot about Alistair and what happened between you. It's been six years. You need to move on.'

'I did move on and I think now it's pretty clear…' she glanced over at Georgie and Ned to make her point '…that I have to do it again.'

She saw the realisation in her sister's eyes. 'You slept with him! That's why you're so hurt. That's it. Time for action.'

'What are you going to do?' She was wary. Subtlety wasn't Tori's strong point.

'Call off Georgie. I'm going to give you a fighting chance.'

'You can't tell her to back off in front of Ned!'

'Why not?'

'Because you look exactly like me and he'll suspect something,' she pointed out dryly.

'Is that your only objection?'

Sarah grimaced. 'Embarrassingly enough, yes. I

have no objection to someone else getting rid of Georgie, even if it does nothing to change my predicament.'

'OK, then, I'll get Hattie to do the dirty work. It's my party after all.'

She left with a wave of her hand before Sarah could double-check whether she really meant to send Hattie to speak to Georgie.

Part of her was ready to curl up with humiliation. Another part was punching the air that at the very least Ned wouldn't be going home with gorgeous, smug Georgie.

Not tonight anyway.

Ned had been nursing his beer, an expensive one. No surprises there. Revamped pubs and inflated prices went hand in hand. He'd been looking into the amber liquid, wondering how long he'd have to stay with his mates for the sake of appearances, eager to cut and run as soon as he could, when a bubbly blonde bounced up to him, apparently thrilled to see him.

He been about to drain his glass and make his excuses but instead he now found himself ordering 'Georgie' champagne as she flirted with him.

He knew the routine. He'd played the game before so he answered the questions she asked in the lilting, slightly childlike voice that women seemed to use at this stage of the getting-to-know-you game. He picked up on her body language which she was working to the hilt—looking up at him with wide eyes through thick lashes, tilting her body towards him at the pelvis, mini-mising the space between them as she closed her eyes briefly to sip from her glass and swallow deeply.

Normally he loved all that. But tonight he was simply going through the motions. Tonight the magic was missing. And that was bothering him more than he wanted to admit because he had a hunch it had nothing to do with Georgie and everything to do with him.

Georgie was the epitome of his ideal woman. She was blonde and cute with more than her fair share of cleavage, and she was very, very impressed with him. But something wasn't right and he knew what it was.

She wasn't Sarah.

But he couldn't have Sarah.

He'd spent three days trying to reconcile himself with the idea that Sarah had his little brother's heart. Three days trying to come to terms with the facts. But the facts were what they were. He'd long since come to terms with the deaths of his brother and father and he didn't mind the idea of them being organ donors but he knew that was in theory. When he was hit with the reality that the girl he was sleeping with had his brother's heart, well, that was something else altogether.

So he and Sarah were history. He had to get over her. Sitting beside him was a gorgeous woman, one who ordinarily would have no trouble capturing his attention, so he would try to put thoughts of Sarah aside and concentrate a bit harder on Georgie. Perhaps then the old magic would kick in.

She was certainly giving him every sign she was interested. She'd swivelled around on her stool and was leaning right in now, her knee pushing between his knees, as she gazed up at him, her lips parted, her eyes wide.

She was definitely interested and he checked his

reaction. Nothing. Not a thing. While Georgie tossed her blonde hair and gazed at him with blue eyes, all he wished for was a brunette with grey eyes in her place. If he closed his eyes he could imagine Sarah sitting in Georgie's place. She wouldn't be using the usual feminine flirting tools to capture his attention; she wouldn't need to. All she'd need to do would be to look his way and the sparks they were able to generate would take care of the rest. Ned felt a stirring in his groin as the memory of the one night they'd had together surfaced.

Obviously it was going to take more than Georgie to get him through this, and as he was wondering exactly what it would take, Georgie's friend Hattie appeared beside them. She apologised to him as she whispered in Georgie's ear, glancing at him all the while. Something was up. Georgie went from looking flirty and fun to sulky and put-out in one second flat.

Hattie scuttled off, and Georgie disentangled herself with a great show of reluctance from her resting place between his legs, leaving one hand high up on his inner thigh in demonstration of where she'd rather stay. 'Apparently I have to go.'

She sniffed, her annoyance plain in her tone. But he wasn't about to ask her to stay. He didn't want her to. Not tonight.

Maybe he'd run into her again and maybe next time he'd be back to his old self. From the flirty way she glanced back at him over her shoulder and from the way she worked her hips in her snug jeans as she tottered away, he got the feeling she'd be happy to see him again.

But tonight his heart wasn't in it.

CHAPTER EIGHT

'HAPPY birthday to you, happy birthday to you…'

Men were crowded around the table in the mess room, singing with gusto as they presented Ned with his birthday cake. He did his best to look pleased while he wished the alarm would sound, calling them to an emergency. He had never felt less like celebrating a birthday before.

Finally the song ended, someone passed him a knife and instructed him to cut the cake. 'Don't touch the plate or your wish won't come true.'

Sarah.

Her name rushed up from his subconscious. In the week since he'd seen her, he'd done his best not to think about her but she was constantly popping up in his thoughts. Yet what was the point of that? There was no point. Thinking about her, seeing her, would achieve nothing. Not when there was no possible way to reconcile her past with his.

He cut the cake, the ever-hungry fire crew grabbing the pieces as soon as they were served, and picked up a fork, ready to tackle a piece himself, attempting to get into the spirit of the day while wondering how he could possibly eat when he felt as though his stomach had lodged in his throat.

As he brought the fork to his mouth, the siren sounded and the station lights began to flash.

'Attention, Attention, HAZMAT team responding to a scene of unknown contamination. Repeat HAZMAT unit responding to a CBR incident.'

The crew immediately looked to Ned for confirmation, suspecting it was another practice run for the team of first responders.

Ned dropped the fork to his plate and jumped to his feet. 'It's not a drill, guys, this is the real thing.'

They were about to find out how well prepared they were to tackle chemical, biological and radiation hazards.

Slices of cake and cups of coffee were abandoned on the mess table as the team left the room. Within seconds they'd slid down the pole and were pulling on their boots before climbing into the appliance. The station lights were flashing, the doors were open and the commuting traffic came to a standstill for the appliances to pull out of the building.

As Station Officer, Ned sat in the front passenger seat while Tony drove the HAZMAT truck. Ned switched on the mobile data terminal, getting confirmation of their destination. Information flashed up on the small computer screen attached to the dashboard.

'We're heading for the velodrome,' he told Tony.

'The first stage of the international cycling protour? Man, that's huge. It's going to be a mess if this is the real thing. There'll be thousands there.'

'Including, to complicate matters, international

media, all there before us to cover it.' From what Ned had read in the paper, the event was primarily a PR exercise with autograph and photo opportunities and a chance for major sponsors to get some publicity prior to the first stage of the race, which was due to begin the following day.

They pulled out of the station, turned right and were closely followed by another fire appliance and two ambulances. In normal traffic the journey would take fifteen minutes.

He was aiming to do it in less than ten.

The traffic cleared from their path as they turned north, siren blaring. As they sped through the streets Ned gathered as much information as he could. The main event was being staged in and around the streets of Adelaide, using city and country roads, but today's event was a warm-up, using the velodrome.

From the information coming through the MDT it seemed as though something had been released into the velodrome, something that was affecting a large number of the three thousand spectators and competitors. There were reports of unusual respiratory and visual symptoms being suffered by cyclists and spectators alike. What had caused the symptoms was unclear, as was how the exposure had occurred, but it was possible something had been released through the air-conditioning system.

Whether it was a deliberate act of terrorism, an accident or an attention-grabbing exercise, no one knew. And from the point of view of the fire service at this stage, it was irrelevant. Whatever the cause, Ned was responsible for controlling the scene, limiting any spread of contamination and minimising casualties. Only the outcome was important.

'Tell your officers to secure the area, get people out of the velodrome into fresh air but don't let them leave the vicinity. It's imperative we contain any contamination. Our ETA is two minutes.' Ned issued radio instructions to the traffic police as the convoy of emergency vehicles hurtled towards the velodrome. The HAZMAT truck was being followed by several fire appliances from the metropolitan service and the country fire service; ambulances, state emergency services vehicles and police cars completed the procession.

Tony turned off the main road and along the service road leading to the velodrome. On Ned's direction, he stopped the appliance so they could suit up into the HAZMAT overalls before continuing to the venue. Hordes of people were gathering on the lawns in front of the building and the size of the crowd pleased Ned as it appeared most people had been able to get out of the venue. He hoped that would translate into minimal casualties.

He scanned the set-up. To his right was the velodrome car park, so full there was no chance of commandeering it. To his left was an open paddock, where nothing was growing. It was a dusty allotment, full of dead weeds. Not a scenic spot but it would suit his purposes perfectly. In front of him lay the velodrome. It had one main entrance that opened onto an expansive lawn where people were gathering. So far it seemed as though the police had managed to contain the crowd and prevent them from getting through to the car park. The fire exits would be operational, though, so some people would be on the other side of the velodrome, out of sight. They would have to be brought round to this side.

Tony stopped the appliance again at Ned's sign, and Ned jumped out and began to direct the other emergency services vehicles to their locations. He sent the ambulances to the lawns; triage would be set up there. He directed two MFS appliances further ahead along the service road, uphill and upwind of the velodrome, instructing them to park on the edge of the vacant paddock and set up in a side-by-side formation ready to begin decontamination showers. The other vehicles pulled in behind the HAZMAT truck.

The crews of first responders swarmed out of their vehicles and Ned knew without looking that the crowd would be staring. As a group, the crews in their white overalls, complete with full face masks and hoods, looked bizarre, a squadron of astronauts descending on the velodrome. There was a risk that the sight of the emergency teams completely covered up would cause panic, making it imperative to get the crowd informed and controlled as quickly as possible.

Approaching the traffic policeman who had been holding the fort—Officer O'Reilly, according to his badge—Ned introduced himself and got straight to the point.

'What have we got?'

'Total crowd of about three thousand people and, at a guess, one third of those seem to have been affected by something—they think something came through the air-conditioning ducts.'

'Has the air-conditioning been shut down?'

No one seemed to know. Ned was pleased to see the

first responders, including the paramedic and police liaison people, heading his way. He needed to get things happening, he needed the crews to get things under control. He pointed at people as they arrived beside him, rapidly issuing instructions, relieved that the simulated exercise had only recently taken place. It meant protocol would be fresh in people's minds and they'd be more confident in dealing with the confusion and enormity of the situation.

'Tony, you and Paul get inside, shut down the air-con and check for any casualties. Jim and TJ, check the perimeter of the velodrome. Officer O'Reilly, what symptoms are people reporting?'

'Respiratory distress, blurred vision with teary eyes, nausea, vomiting. No fatalities that we know of.'

'Any loss of consciousness?' The paramedic liaison, Angie, asked that question.

Officer O'Reilly shook his head. 'Nothing's been reported and I haven't seen anything.'

'Any ideas about what we're dealing with?' Ned turned to Angie.

'Most likely a chemical of some description. Whether it's been deliberately released is probably not significant. We can treat the symptoms, but we need to find out what it is in terms of longer-term consequences.'

Ned took Angie's idea on board and continued to issue instructions. 'Alex, check the HAZMAT register and report back with any likely chemicals. Angie, send your guys into the crowd to triage, treat anyone who's urgent, but any civilian who can manage it needs to be sent through the showers, in their underwear, then they can seek treatment if necessary.'

He turned to address his police liaison officer next. 'Lucas, we'll need male and female tents so people can remove their underwear after they've showered. We'll need to give them gowns or blankets and your officers will have to be responsible for triple-bagging and tagging people's personal possessions. Form a corral to direct people to the appliances so they can be hosed down and we'll have to set up another assembly point past the showers and tents. Once people have been cleared through decontamination get your guys to direct them through the tents for fresh clothes and then you can sort them out for evacuation, statements or further medical help. Get the medicos to determine who needs treatment.'

Ned held out his hand for the megaphone Lucas was holding and brought it to his mouth to address the crowd.

'Can I have everyone's attention? I'm Station Officer Ned Kellaway from the Metropolitan Fire Service and I'll be in charge of your evacuation. There is a protocol that needs to be followed so please listen carefully.' He spoke slowly, loudly and intentionally used his deepest speaking voice. 'We are dealing with a suspected chemical leak. Some people are experiencing breathing difficulties. If you are feeling unwell or having trouble breathing, please wait where you are.' Again, he emphasised the crucial words. 'Wait where you are. The paramedics are moving among you and they will assist you. Those of you who are able, please make your way towards the two fire engines on my left. You must all be hosed down to remove any contamination from your skin and clothes. It is extremely important that you don't leave the area until you have completed the decontamination process.'

The two fire engines he'd referred to were parked parallel to each other and had their fire hoses turned on, their sprays intercepting at forty-five degrees in a huge water display, spectacular against the clear blue sky. It also made it easy for the crowd to see where to head. At least it was a warm day; being hosed down in cold water wasn't the most pleasant of experiences.

He put the megaphone on the ground beside him before repositioning his mask and stood, watching as the police started to direct the crowd. He needed to know from Alex what, if any, hazardous chemicals were stored on the site.

Sarah was in the first wave of doctors to arrive at the velodrome. Three thousand potential casualties was a huge number to deal with. There was no way the paramedics could handle anywhere close to that number alone. The doctors, covered in protective overalls, hoods and masks, raced past the stationary vehicles to the lawns in front of the velodrome.

Hurrying past two huge fire trucks—'appliances', she mentally corrected herself—she saw the CFS crews setting up tents and paramedics establishing a medical zone. She continued towards the centre of the operation, knowing she'd most likely find Ned when she got there and reminding herself that what had happened between them was irrelevant. For now, at least.

As she got closer she heard Ned's voice over the loudhailer, slightly distorted but still easily recognizable, and she listened closely. She needed to know what they were dealing with. She heard 'difficulty breathing' and she could see paramedics moving among the crowd, starting to treat people. That's where she needed to be.

To do that, she needed to find Angie and get her orders, but she couldn't see her in the chaos. She could see Ned, the logical person to check in with, and when she saw him put the loudhailer down and unclip his two-way radio, she headed over.

'Ned, it's Jim. Come in. Over.'

'Go ahead, Jim. Over.'

'We need a medic to the north-eastern boundary. We've found the source of the contamination and we have two men needing urgent help. Severe respiratory distress.'

'I've got it.' Sarah had heard the conversation and caught Ned's eye, giving him a thumbs-up sign to re-confirm she'd take the call. He returned the sign, not answering as he was still on the radio, but he did nod and was that a half-smile?

She wasn't certain but at least he'd acknowledged her. She picked up her medical kit and took off for the velodrome. After seeing him at the pub, charming Georgie as if there was no tomorrow, she'd wondered if he'd even bother to say hello the next time they met. She was inexplicably pleased he had and then irritated with herself that it mattered. She'd wanted to matter much, much more than she did, and that wasn't going to happen.

Moving at a rapid pace towards the northern side of the velodrome, she could hear someone hot on her heels. As she stopped to commandeer a portable oxygen supply from a paramedic, Ned overtook her and she found that now she was following him to the site. When she got there, he was in position on the north-eastern side of the velodrome, right next to the metal doors leading to the power and electrical units. He was crouched beside two prostrate figures. The two first responders who'd radioed in the situation were digging a hole and in the background was a utility truck, loaded with wooden beams, bags of concrete and various tools and equipment. Squatting down beside Ned, she placed the oxygen tank on the ground as she struggled to regain her breath. She wasn't fit enough to run around in the cumbersome biohazard suit, lugging an oxygen tank and a medical kit. It didn't escape her notice that Ned was barely puffing.

There was no time for pleasantries and the way she was feeling, she wouldn't have had any at her disposal anyway.

'My name is Sarah,' she said to the first man. 'I'm a doctor. I'm going to give you oxygen to help you breathe.' She connected the masks and slipped them onto their faces before attaching oximeters to their fingers.

'What's happened?' she asked Ned, continuing to work while listening to his description of events.

'There's an old forty-four-gallon drum buried under here. It looks like these guys were doing some maintenance or building work and we suspect they've accidentally punctured the drum. These guys are having so much trouble breathing they can't talk. Jim and TJ are trying to uncover more of the drum to see if it's got a label on it.'

Both patients' faces were grey and although their pupils weren't dilated, their eyes were teary. Their breathing was shallow and rapid but there was no sign that either of them had vomited, which meant that anything they'd inhaled or ingested was still in their systems. That wasn't good.

'I see something.' TJ stopped digging and lay on the ground to rub dirt from the side of the drum, fully exposing a stencilled label. 'Chloropicrin.'

Not good. 'Chloropicrin was used as a chemical weapon in the First World War. What's it doing here?'

'There used to be market gardens around here. Chloropicrin was also used as a soil sterilizing agent and for fumigating rats. There could be lots of this buried around here,' Ned said. He looked at her properly now, for the first time since this incident had begun, but he was still looking at her as if she was just any medic who happened to be here. Nothing more. 'What needs to be done?' he asked her, and she knew what he was really asking—how bad is this?

It was about as bad as it could be for the two workmen lying at her feet, but for those inside the velodrome she hoped it wouldn't be as grim. She opened a bottle of saline solution as she spoke and started to rinse the workmen's faces.

'The vapours would have been sucked into the velodrome through the air-conditioning. The contamination will depend on where people were sitting and how quickly they were evacuated. Eyes and airways will be mainly affected. Eyes can be washed and if people are mainly experiencing stinging eyes and a bit of nausea then the concentration of vapours hopefully wasn't too high. Get everyone rinsed off and anyone with breathing difficulties or a history of asthma or other respiratory problems needs to be seen by one of the medical team. Urgently.'

'And these two?' Ned glanced down.

Sarah gave a very slight shake of her head. 'They need to get to hospital. I can't do anything more for them here.' She doubted that the hospital would be able to save them either. High levels of chloropicrin could be fatal when inhaled, but she couldn't say that now. She'd get in contact with the men's employer—someone would need to contact their next of kin and ensure they got to the hospital as a matter of urgency. There wasn't much more that could be done.

Ned nodded, letting her know he'd interpreted her body language. She continued to do what she could for the men as she listened to Ned take control. He called for an ambulance, notified the team about the chemical involved, passed on Sarah's instructions about anyone with respiratory symptoms and then instructed Jim and TJ to get the drum kit and patch the hole to get the drum properly sealed.

'Anything else?' he queried as he finished.

'We've got things under control. You go and do what you need to.'

Sarah watched him leave, watched as he dodged an ambulance as it pulled up alongside the patients. There'd been no obvious awkwardness between them but, then, they were both professionals and had jobs to do.

It didn't mean anything had changed.

It didn't mean they had a future.

He'd rejected her and she needed to move on. She would move on.

paramedics had the ambulance doors open. She
entrated on handing over her patients. Thoughts of
d didn't have a place in her life today.

Ned headed for the makeshift showers, planning on
checking the progress of the decontamination routine.
The spray from the fire hoses looked very dramatic, col-
liding in mid-air and raining down on the pathway
between the appliances, soaking everyone as they
walked along the corridor. Fully clothed but carrying
their shoes, the cyclists and spectators then headed for
the tents at the far end of the showers where they would
be given dry gowns or blankets before being organised
for evacuation.

He was still several feet from the appliances when a
loud explosion ripped through the air. The ground
beneath his feet trembled as many people, already on
edge, screamed with fright.

Sarah?

The explosion had been behind him. Had Jim or TJ
accidentally punctured another drum? Would it ex-
plode? Ned had no idea but his first thought was for
Sarah. Turning on his heel, he sprinted through the
grounds as best he could back to the velodrome, trying
to reach Jim on the two-way as he ran.

'Jim, this is Ned. What happened? Over.'

'An oxygen tank rolled out of the ambulance and got
its top knocked off…'

Ned was back on the scene before Jim could finish
his reply. He scanned the grounds, hoping for the best
but terrified he'd be confronted with more injuries from
a wayward oxygen cylinder turned missile.

At first glance he counted six people, where there should be seven. He checked again—Jim plus two paramedics working on the two injured workmen and TJ beyond them, still working on the drum.

Six.

Where was the seventh?

Where was Sarah?

He scanned the ground and saw she was separate from the group, picking herself up gingerly from the ground. Was she hurt?

'Sarah?' His heart was in his throat. As he reached her she sat up in the dirt and rubbed her knee. 'Are you OK?' He put a hand under her elbow, helping her to her feet, but she brushed his hand away.

'I'm fine. I just had to dive out of the way of the cylinder. I just got a bit winded, that's all.' She looked to her left and he followed her gaze and saw a large dent in the doors of the plant room. The cylinder was lying on the ground where it had fallen after crashing into the metal doors.

'Why didn't someone help you?'

'I indicated I was OK. They all need to keep going with what they're doing. I told you, I'm just winded.' She was simultaneously trying to rub her knee where she must have taken the brunt of her landing and catch her breath, all the while glancing at the patients, clearly impatient to get back in the fray. As he knew he should, too.

As the paramedics began lifting the workmen onto stretchers, he knew he had no reason to stay. It was all under control. The problem was, the way he felt was anything but under control. He had no idea what that meant. All he knew was he felt as if he'd been on the receiving end of the oxygen cylinder missile.

Sarah had come close to being seriously injured, even killed. When a valve got knocked off the end of a gas cylinder, it turned it into a lethal projectile. She'd had a near miss. How would he have felt if she hadn't been so lucky?

She nodded a farewell at him, her mouth set in a line rather than turning up in the smile he so adored. Her face gave nothing away as she turned her back to him and limped back to the patients. Someone watching would be hard-pressed to guess whether they knew one another.

He forced himself to pick up his two-way and broadcast the all-clear. He had to get back to the crowd to make sure there were no signs of developing hysteria.

And when this was all over, he had to work out what the hell had just happened to him. His chest felt tight, constricted, and he was struggling to take a decent breath. The feeling brought back memories of his early childhood, fighting for a deep breath, struggling for air. Swimming had taught him how to breathe correctly, how to relax his diaphragm so he wasn't fighting for oxygen, and he'd forgotten what it was like to labour for a breath.

What had brought this sensation back?

Ned turned his head sharply to his right as he caught a glimpse of a slim brunette in his peripheral vision. Once again, it wasn't Sarah. All day he'd sighted her, or women he'd mistaken for her, as though the universe was sending him subliminal messages.

He rubbed one hand across his eyes. Yesterday's drama at the velodrome had obviously taken its toll and weariness was making him imagine things. He ran a hand through his hair and kept on walking, returning to the fire station after a meeting in the city. He stopped at a corner, waiting for the lights to change, and realised he was in front of the building that housed the organ donor foundation offices. He'd known the offices were here, he'd seen their sign before, but had he unintentionally come this way, sensing the answers to his continuing confusion might lie here?

Hesitating, he was about to walk on when someone brushed past him, making the glass doors slide open. For a moment he assumed he was seeing mirages again but, no, this time, she was real.

'Sarah?'

Even as he called her name he realised he wasn't seeing Sarah but rather a woman who was her spitting image. As she turned to face him, he realised his sixth sense was right. Her posture was different and so were her clothes. Sarah would never wear such a low-cut top. The top itself wasn't overly revealing. It had a simple V-neck but it was low enough to expose the shiny silver scar running between her breasts.

The slim brunette looked him up and down unashamedly, taking in the uniform. She extended her hand for him to shake and said, 'Hello, Ned.'

He blinked, trying to work out how this Sarah-impersonator knew him. While he stood there, running through scenarios, the girl continued.

'I'm Tori, Sarah's twin.'

He hadn't realised Sarah was an identical twin, identical right down to their scars. Had Sarah told him and he hadn't listened?

He shook his head, trying to clear the fog from his brain. 'How did you know me?'

The twitch around the corners of her lips, as though she was fighting back a smile, suggested she'd seen him before, he just didn't know it. 'A lucky guess,' was all she said, and went on, 'You looked like you were just coming in. Have you got an appointment?'

'I'm not actually sure what I'm doing here.'

'Then you're looking for a chat. People who hover on the doorstep only do that if they need someone to talk to who understands.'

He grinned at her then. 'Are you in sales? You make a good pitch.'

'In a way.' She was smiling broadly at him, Sarah's smile. Or at least the smile he'd done such a fine job of wiping off her face. 'I'm a counsellor here. It just so happens it's my lunch-break.' she waved the paper bag she was carrying. 'And it's also true that I listen better when I'm eating. Less chance for me to interrupt.' She was laughing now. 'So come on in and let's get to know each other.'

She stepped back on the threshold, the doors slid open but he couldn't follow. 'Tori,' he called her back. 'That would be too weird, chatting to you. You're Sarah's sister.'

'Whatever I hear in these four walls stays in these four walls. But no pressure, you can book and see someone else. It's just that the hardest part about seeing someone is turning up.' She shrugged. 'You've done that. It'd be a shame to have to turn up all over again without learning there's nothing to be scared of. Or you can chat to me as someone who'll listen. You don't have to see me as a counsellor. Lots of the time all we need is someone to listen without putting their two cents in to work out how we feel.' She waved a hand around expansively. 'It's my lunch-break after all, I don't have to clock on as such, and it'll still stay between you and me.' Once again, she looked him up and down, before adding with an impish grin, 'Like I said, I'll be eating, so I can't interrupt. Do I have a sale?'

Ned extended his hand, taking hers in a firm shake. 'Sold.' The twitch at the corners of her lips turned upwards into a smile, approval shining in her eyes.

And thirty minutes later he'd amazed himself by forgetting it was Sarah's sister he was spilling his life history to. He was talking, really talking, and things were coming out of his mouth he'd never in his wildest dreams thought about, tapping into the fears and terror of a little boy whose life had been ripped apart by one phone call the night his little brother and the centre of his universe, his dad, had been killed.

As he talked, he was drawn deeper and deeper into memories that had lain undisturbed for many years. Bent over his knees as he sat in a low armchair, he was vaguely aware he was hunkered down, gazing intently at the floor, as if the memories were etched into the carpet.

'I was terrified, I can feel it, here.' He touched his chest. 'Like I stopped breathing, as if I couldn't breathe no matter how hard I tried.' He paused, gulped for air, the connection not lost on him and presumably not on Tori. Closing his eyes, he concentrated on forcing himself to breathe normally. It was an incredible struggle. 'I can remember how I felt when I was little. When I heard. I simply started holding my breath, not wanting to take another lungful of air in case it hurt worse than the one before it.' He shook his head, overwhelmed as the memories returned and, with the benefit of hindsight and an adult mind, reassembled themselves into a meaningful pattern. 'And all these years, I've thought I'd dealt with it fine, assumed that kids just pick themselves up and move on, that they're oblivious to the trauma. I just blocked it out.' He blinked, hard, and felt himself rising up out of that strange place between memory and the present.

'You blocked it out but you're still carrying the fear and pain?'

'In a nutshell.' He rubbed his eyes and shook his head free of the last vestiges of painful memory. 'You're good at this,' he said, and finally he raised his head and looked at her, bringing himself firmly back into the present. 'You should think about being a counsellor.'

She smiled but didn't bite—she was too good at what she did to be distracted by a wisecrack. 'What impact do you think your reaction to your loss has had on you?'

'I think I've thought as long as I didn't get close to someone, I'd be able to breathe.' And just like that, he dropped the bombshell of insight into his life. How could it be that easy? Yet it had just come, unbidden.

She let him sit with that thought, he could see her doing it, but he didn't know why. Until he looked at Tori, Sarah's other half, and the penny dropped. 'Until Sarah. I could breathe when I let Sarah close.'

'And now?'

'Yesterday, at the velodrome...' He glanced at Tori,

assuming she knew about the drama of the previous day. She nodded and he continued, 'I thought Sarah had been hurt, seriously injured, and since then I've had that tightness in my chest again, like it hurts to breathe.'

'And what does that mean?'

He took another steadying lungful of air. He looked Tori squarely in the eye. 'That means I'm front-runner to take the prize for biggest dope of the year. I latched onto the connection with Danny because it's what I do, I keep my distance. Sarah had already got me, and I panicked and used that. And the connection between Danny and Sarah was uncomfortable, challenging even, but if I hadn't been so scared of being close to someone, I would've worked through it. Instead, I simply seized the idea and told both of us it meant the end.'

'And does it?'

'It's still weird. But all I know is, since I met Sarah, I can breathe properly. And since I've lost her, I can't. It's surreal.'

'Surreal?'

'That losing Danny would make me stop breathing and losing Sarah would do the same thing, and then Sarah has Danny's heart.'

'Is it Danny's heart?' She let the words drop quietly into the space between them. 'Or Sarah's?' She raised grey eyes to meet his, a gentle challenge implicit deep within them.

'Every beat is pumping Sarah's blood around her body and keeping her alive.' Again, the clarity with which the answers were presenting themselves in his mind was so stunning he just couldn't believe he hadn't worked this out in two seconds flat. 'It's Sarah's.'

'Sarah's?'

He shrugged. It was a no-brainer. Whose heart could it be but the person it was keeping alive? 'The gift was Danny's and my mum's. The heart is Sarah's.'

Which left only one vital question: was it a heart he wanted to win?

CHAPTER NINE

IF YESTERDAY hadn't been the worst day of her life so far, it came pretty darned close. Having to deal with two fatal injuries, three thousand potential victims and Ned had pushed her beyond her limits. She needed a holiday. Once Tori's wedding was over, that's just what she'd do. Go away and lie on a beach somewhere. And not get up for anything.

Right now, a cup of tea would just have to do instead. There were two letters propped up against the kettle for her. Tori obviously wanted her to see them. Both were from the foundation.

She chose one and slit it open as she flicked the kettle on. This one informed her she'd been the successful bidder on a silent auction item at the foundation dinner, her credit card had been charged and would she please call to arrange collection of her prize?

Memories of that night swamped her. She'd left before the auction had concluded. She may well have been kissing Ned when the final bids had been called, oblivious to the fact she was just about to fall in love, swiftly moving on to have her heart broken. Well, more fool her.

With thoughts of Ned foremost in her mind, she opened the second letter.

'*Dear Dr Richardson,*' she read, '*We regret to inform you that your donor's family has requested to maintain anonymity at this time. We are therefore unable to pass your details on to them. We will retain your request on file and if, in the future, your donor's family changes its request, we will contact you again.*'

Sarah frowned and reread the letter. It didn't make any more sense the second time. Ned and his mum already knew about her. Why would they send this letter?

The penny dropped.

Ned had cancelled the consent.

Could he do that?

Obviously he could and he had. He'd acted like he still cared a little yesterday, seeming worried about her after the oxygen cylinder had exploded. Clearly it was all part of his ingrained charm. 'Glad I've wised up enough not to start thinking his attitude yesterday meant a change of heart about us,' she muttered, aiming to feel pleased with her progress but only managing to feel hurt and disappointed all over again.

The kettle switched off just as the phone began to ring. She debated letting the answering-machine pick up so she could avoid talking to anyone but relented at the last second in case it was related to Tori's imminent wedding. Tucking the receiver between her ear and chin, she managed to pour water from the kettle at the same time.

'May I speak to Sarah Richardson, please?' asked a woman's voice, rich and well modulated.

'Speaking.'

'Ah.' There was a pause before the woman continued. 'I don't really know where to start. I'm Joan Kellaway. I'm—'

'Ned's mother,' Sarah interrupted. Her glance went straight to the letter she'd just received. Why was she ringing now?

'I hope you don't mind me calling,' Ned's mother went on, unperturbed at Sarah's brusqueness. 'Normally I would have written to you but I thought, since you know Ned and you know what's happened…' She cut herself off, obviously collecting her thoughts. 'Anyway, the organ donor foundation gave me your number—'

'Why would they do that?' Sarah interrupted again. 'I've just received a letter saying you didn't want any contact.'

'Pardon?' Joan sounded puzzled.

'I've just read it not one minute ago. It says, "your donor's family has requested to maintain anonymity at this time."'

'There must be some mistake, my instructions were quite clear and I haven't changed them.'

'Somebody has.'

'I know Ned wouldn't have and there's no one else who'd have authority.'

Sarah's heart softened a little at the reminder that this woman had lost both her husband and her younger son. Sarah had only lost her pride and her heart.

Joan continued, 'He was certainly not that comfortable with me going down this path, but he's been supportive and he wouldn't have changed my instructions. He's far too considerate for that.'

Sarah bit her tongue and refrained from asking

whether they were talking about the same Ned Kellaway. 'I'm not claiming to know how it happened, I'm just telling you what *has* happened.'

'There's obviously been a communication mix-up somewhere and I'll sort it out. I can hear you're upset and I can understand why, but the fact is, I would very much like to meet you.' She paused, then added, 'If you haven't changed your mind.'

How much did Joan know about her son's relationship with Sarah? The uncertainty in her tone when she'd asked her last question suggested she was worried Sarah would refuse contact because Ned had ended their involvement. She pondered it for a moment, then surprised herself by saying, 'I haven't changed my mind. I'd like to meet you too.' She heard Joan breath a sigh of relief and Sarah added, 'But it's my sister's wedding in two days and I'm pushed for time. Perhaps I could ring you in a few days?'

'Of course, you must be frantic, getting ready, but what a happy time.' Once more there was an undertone of sadness beneath the genuine warmth in her voice. This time Sarah thawed enough to feel sure she'd like Joan. Even if she was Ned's mum. 'Is your sister older or younger than you?'

'She's my twin.'

'Even more exciting. Is this the first wedding in your family?'

'Absolutely. There's just the two of us and our mother has gone totally over the top. I guess that's understandable, given she never thought she'd see this day.' From being stand-offish, Sarah was now conscious she was babbling to a total stranger. It could only be the stress of the past twenty-four hours combined with the pleasant nature of Joan affecting her.

'Do you mind me asking why they never thought they'd see your sister married?'

'It was touch and go with both of us when we were born. We both had the same heart condition, we both needed transplants.'

'Both of you! Can I ask what for?'

Sarah knew instinctively that Joan was gathering the information she'd been keen to have all these years. Had agreeing to donate Danny's organs been the right thing to do? Had lives been saved and changed and made better?

'We had a condition called hypoplastic left heart syndrome.' Giving Joan some information now was a small gift in return for the generous gift she herself had received all those years before. There was no need to make her wait until they met face to face. 'The left sides of our hearts didn't develop properly.'

'Transplants were the only option?'

'The doctors tried a different surgical procedure but that didn't work very well for either of us so Tori had her transplant when she was almost two. Mine happened when I was three.'

Joan was silent for a moment before asking, 'And you've not had problems since then, in all these years?'

'We're twenty-eight—next month, in fact—and neither of us have had any complications. We were very lucky.'

'Sarah, I really appreciate you taking the time to share this with me now. I'll give you my number and when you're ready, I'd love to meet you and talk some more.'

Sarah wrote down the number, said goodbye and

hung up, feeling much calmer than when she'd read the letter. Something had fallen into place during that phone call. Ned's mother sounded nice and she'd be quite happy now to meet her. She'd been dreading having to meet Ned's mum since things had gone sour with Ned but now, having spoken with her, she knew that meeting her would be her gift of thanks to her donor's mum. It wasn't something she needed to do for herself.

And what about Ned?

She hadn't really considered Ned's point of view until now. She'd been far too busy wrapped up in her own disappointment and hurt.

She was clear about this much at least: Ned hadn't wanted to know about the recipient. Like her, he didn't need to know. Yet with the discovery of the links between the families, he'd been forced into a position of *having* to know. Not only that. Automatically, by seeing her, he'd have a constant reminder of exactly what he'd steered clear of finding out.

It put a new spin on his reaction. Suddenly she could see it from his angle: finding out the woman he'd just slept with was only alive because she had his dead brother's heart must have been a shock.

Her heart softened a little in his favour, but only a little. She could accept now it might honestly have been too much for him to deal with rather than simply being a convenient excuse to end it with her. She could accept her own insecurities had encouraged her to interpret it in the least favourable light. It was credible that it was only her connection with Danny that had thrown him.

What she couldn't accept was how he'd moved on

so swiftly. If she'd meant anything at all to him, he'd have tried to work through it with her. Instead, he'd moved swiftly to cut all ties. And that night with Georgie at the pub, he'd made it all look so easy. And he'd never wavered. Other than showing concern for her at the HAZMAT scene, he'd obviously found it a cinch to close the door on her and move right on.

The bottom line was she'd fallen for someone who hadn't fallen for her.

She'd never been more than a short-term fling.

'For a smart woman, Sarah Richardson,' she muttered as she tipped her now cold tea down the sink and put the kettle on again, 'you're consistently dense when it comes to men.'

The only bright spot on the horizon was that in two days' time Tori would be married and Sarah would have some free time again.

She planned on using a fair part of it to watch romantic movies and cry her eyes out. Not to mention booking that holiday.

Tori slid behind the wheel of her car just as her mobile started ringing. 'Blast, I'm already late,' she muttered, but she was feeling superstitious enough about her wedding the next morning to be unable to ignore a call. She pushed the answer button. 'Tori here.'

The reason for Ned's call left her flummoxed. She was lost for words for a good ten seconds, recovering her powers of speech in time to pepper him with questions. The answers left her just as gob-smacked as he dropped bombshell after bombshell.

When she'd fired off almost every question in her

armoury, she hit him with the big one: 'Does this change how you feel about Sarah?'

She listened attentively to his answer, attuned to hidden fears and intentions, but all she learned was that he didn't yet know what he wanted. She was pretty sure *she* knew what that was, but he needed more time and telling him would hardly be the professional thing to do. When he'd finished his tale, she said, 'You say you don't want to hurt her, but you already have. So if that's your prime concern, maybe there's nothing to be worried about.'

From his silence, she wasn't sure if he didn't quite get her meaning or was already considering her suggestion. It wouldn't hurt to leave him mulling it over.

She ended the call by reiterating her invitation, saying, 'I'll see you at the church,' leaving her wondering whether she'd just made the right decision.

Her wedding was no time to find out she'd made a total hash of something this important, yet it was what she'd just suggested.

Turning the key in the ignition, she dropped her mobile on the passenger seat, indicated, checked for traffic and pulled out into a gap, suddenly comforted as a thought occurred to her.

No one would criticise on a bride on her wedding day. Not even her sister. Right?

The CBR debriefing session had started at ten on Saturday morning and as the hours ticked by, Ned was growing increasingly impatient and eager to make a run for it. If he missed the wedding, it'd be another night at least before he would have a chance to set things straight. It had already been four days since he'd last seen Sarah, and he wasn't willing to wait another one if he could help it.

The meeting finished in the nick of time, and five and a half hours after it had begun, he burst through the front door of his mum's house, the place he was temporarily still calling home.

'You look lovely,' he said to his mum as he dashed past her in the hall to change, calling back over his shoulder, 'I won't be long.'

Five minutes later, they were in the car and heading for the church to watch Tori get married.

'Slow down, there's plenty of time.'

'No, Mum, I have a distinct feeling I've been running out of time for a while now. Who knows when my chance will be gone?' Silently, he added what he feared, *If it hasn't already.*

They sent each other a sidelong glance and true to her wise nature, she simply gave him an encouraging smile and said, 'I'm sure you've got it all under control. You always have had, you know.'

'I don't think I have half as much as I've convinced myself.'

They drove the rest of the short distance in silent contemplation. There was a very real risk he was too late, if he'd ever really had a chance. But his slight struggle for breath, the tightness in his chest, ever-present since the HAZMAT disaster, made it clear he had no choice. He had to tell Sarah the truth, the whole truth. About so many things. He had a feeling of dread that it all hung on the order in which he told her, and he couldn't decipher which order was the right one and which the kiss of death.

He dropped his mum off at the front of the church before driving off to park the car. He intended to wait outside. Tori had invited them both to the church but he was worried about Sarah's reaction if she saw him and he didn't want to ruin her enjoyment of the wedding. His mission would be better accomplished if she was happy.

He wandered back to wait under the shade of the presbytery verandah, his view of the church partially obscured by bushes. He saw the wedding car arrive and the two women and an older man emerge. Ned glanced at Tori and although he knew she looked fabulous, he only had eyes for Sarah.

In a dark dress overlaid with some sort of floaty fabric that may or may not have been deep blue, and with her lips painted deep red, she looked amazing. Her hair was loose and a little tousled, in stark contrast to how she normally wore it—bundled neatly into a knot at the base of her neck or in a ponytail. The loose waves evoked memories of her time with him. Before he'd blown it.

An image of her asleep in his bed on the one night they'd had together stirred to life, taunting him. Her hair had been spread across his pillow, loose like it was now, a slight curl through its length. He'd run his fingers through it as she'd slept and he'd marvelled at the feel of it, the look of its soft darkness against her pale breasts.

Now, as then, there was nothing to distract from the simplicity of her appearance: no necklace about her neck, no bracelets. Sarah to a T. Honest, sincere and beautiful, inside and out. She was straightening her sister's dress, fixing her train just so, bending and moving while she focused on Tori. Her movements were lithe and easy, reminiscent of a dancer's grace, and another memory of her in his bed blazed in his mind. How Sarah's warm body, soft in all the right places, had wound about his and how they'd fitted together so well it hurt to think about it.

The bridal party was moving up the steps now, affording him a glimpse of Sarah's slim legs and slim ankles, her feet encased in heels that gave her walk a pleasing lilt. Again, that image of her in his bed, those lean legs wrapped around his torso, flashed before him.

A moment later the trio disappeared from view and he released the breath that, once again, he hadn't known he'd been holding. Dragging in a deep lungful of much-needed air, he started preparing himself to make the most of whatever opportunity he had to speak with her once the ceremony was over. Time was of the essence. A bridesmaid's job was demanding and if he had an opportunity to speak to her, he knew it would be short.

He had to make the most of his chances, because he needed the girl in the dark dress.

The girl who moved as confidently on the dance floor as she did in a disaster zone.

He needed the woman who had disappeared into the church with grace and purpose, her hips moving with a sexy sway beneath her floating dress.

He needed Sarah.

Somewhere between the end of his session with Tori and reaching the front door of the building, he'd been blind-sided by the clear knowledge of what Sarah meant to him. When he'd seen her just now, the truth had hit him again, hard, like a physical blow: he was in love with her.

His eyelids closed as he let himself imagine how she'd feel in his arms, dancing at Tori and Harry's wedding, only emerging from his reverie when he heard the congregation pour out of the church behind the bride and groom. Sarah was attending to Tori's dress again and amidst the crush of onlookers it was hard to see her clearly. Once the cameras finished clicking, capturing pictures of the bridal party, he'd go to her. He didn't want her to see him until it was time. Not that it was likely. The bridal party was completely surrounded by well-wishers. He stepped back further into the shadows, closing his eyes again.

A few minutes later, he felt a touch on his arm. Sarah had come to him.

He opened his eyes.

And cursed his rotten, ill-timed luck.

The click of dozens of cameras rose above the buzz of the wedding guests as Tori stood wrapped in Harry's arms, beaming for the snap-happy crowd. When people started to break the imaginary circle around the bride and groom and swarm forward to congratulate them, Sarah extracted herself from the crowd for a moment's respite.

A moment she knew she would use to return to thoughts of Ned, a useless exercise but one she was rapidly perfecting. Sure, it was madness to waste a thought on him. She'd been nothing but a night of good sex for him. And maybe it had started off as lust for her, too, but she was pretty sure she'd already been his in every sense by the time they'd slept together. This craving she felt for him, this overwhelming need to have him near her, this knowledge that the colour wouldn't come back into her world without him couldn't be explained by lust, no matter how hard she tried.

And, boy, had she been trying.

All these things were real.

She was in love.

She loved Ned.

Scanning the crowd, she tried to breathe in the buzz of happiness and optimism a happy wedding generated. If this had been her wedding…

Drifting into another brief moment of fantasy, her gaze settled on a striking couple and she stared at them for a second or so before she realised who she was looking at.

Ned and Georgie.

Her view wasn't great as they were nestled beyond the crowd in the shadows of the presbytery verandah, but what she saw told her everything she needed to know. Since her phone call with his mum, she'd started seeing things differently. Despite the fact he'd moved on so quickly, she'd had a few stray charitable thoughts about how he'd reacted to the news about Danny. Now she could see he'd not only moved on, he was flaunting the fact. At her sister's wedding.

It was bad enough that Georgie had invited Ned.

But for him to say *yes*?

Did Tori know? Hattie must have known—how could she not have told her?

She caught a glimpse of the purplish-toned tie around Ned's neck. He'd dressed to *match* Georgie?

Georgie in her skimpy lilac dress? The only positive note was that the shade did nothing for her complexion, but from the way she was draped over Ned, she was so close he wouldn't even be able to see what colour she was wearing.

This was the most miserable surprise she'd ever had.

Anger and defiance welled up in her. She wouldn't let them see how much she was hurting. She wouldn't let him see how much she cared.

Head held high, schooling her features into an expression that told the world she was happy, she made a beeline for Harry's best man, the same guy who'd been making unwanted moves on her every time she'd seen him during the wedding preparations.

Right now, as long as talking to him meant avoiding Ned, he was looking like her knight in shining armour.

The next time he found Sarah in the crowd she was being mauled by the best man pretty much in the same manner as Georgie was still pawing him. 'Georgie, come with me.'

Walking as though Georgie wasn't still attached to his arm, he came up behind Sarah and touched her lightly on the shoulder, refusing to lose hope when, on turning and seeing who it was, the light went out of her eyes. When she glanced over and saw Georgie hanging on his arm, the light came back but it told him she was furious. Hopefully what he was about to do would at least take care of that problem.

Ned extended a hand to the best man and, introductions over, pulled Georgie to stand in front of him, saying, 'Scott, this is Georgie. Georgie doesn't have a partner this evening—do you reckon you could keep her company?'

Since Scott was tall, good-looking, smelled of money and looked like he was on the prowl, Ned knew Georgie would get over being foisted off on him. Though, frankly, he didn't much care. He hadn't asked her to come and drape herself over him and create yet one more hurdle between him and Sarah. Scott disappeared with Georgie, hastily, as if worried Ned might reclaim her, leaving Sarah shooting him filthy looks and standing with her slender arms crossed tightly across her chest.

'Sorry about getting rid of Prince Charming, but I have limited time before you need to go and there are things I need to tell you.'

'You don't look in the least bit sorry, you look positively pleased with yourself,' she answered, but the ice had thawed a tiny bit, judging by the glimmer of a smile at the corner of her lovely mouth. He resisted tracing a line around the tantalising curve of her lips, painted an unfamiliar deep red as if to tease him beyond sanity. There'd be time for that later. Lots of time.

'I've gone over and over this, and I don't think there's a perfect way to do it, so I'll just say it.' He filled his lungs with a deep breath and willed the heavens to help him do this right. 'Danny wasn't your donor.' He let that sink in a moment, and then added the rider, 'He was Tori's.'

'What?' Her eyebrows were pulled together, she was frowning, and he knew she was trying to piece the puzzle together at a rapid pace.

'After talking to you, Mum knew something wasn't right. First your letter saying your donor's family didn't want contact, then the dates didn't fit. You had your op months after Danny died. Yesterday she went into the foundation to speak to the supervisor. They worked out that the temp I'd spoken to, the one who told me Danny was your donor, saw "Richardson" and your date of birth on the computer and pulled out your file. It had the right surname and date of birth to match Danny's records and she didn't look further.'

'So…' She was grappling to piece it all together. 'If Danny isn't my donor, then that last letter was correct? My donor's family doesn't want contact?'

'The supervisor wouldn't have given any of your details to Mum so you'll need to double-check, but it looks that way.' He touched her forearm briefly and she pulled away. 'I'm sorry if you won't know your donor's family.'

She cut him off. 'Don't be. I'm not.' She glanced behind him and lifted her hand to signal to someone, before looking back at him. 'It would've been nice to be able to thank them but I don't need to say that if the family doesn't want to hear it. I say my thanks every day anyway. I'm fine with that, and I'm glad it's Tori who found out if it could only be one of us.'

He grimaced. 'So neither of us wanted to know, yet look at the mess it got us into.'

'Mess?'

'That's the second thing I came to tell you. I made a mistake. I let my shock and the fact I'd never wanted to know about Danny's transplant come between us. I should never have let that happen. I'm sorry I did, I'm sorry I hurt you.' He spoke deliberately, not wanting to make a hash of this chance, willing her to hear his sincerity in every word. 'I want to start over.'

'Start over…' She let the phrase hang in the air between them, as though slowly turning it over, looking for holes. There was a confusion of emotions flickering across her face and he knew instinctively this wasn't going to be as easy as saying sorry. 'But that wasn't all that came between us, was it, Ned? Let's face it, you're a short-term kind of guy and I knew that from the start. It's why I let things go as far as they did in the first place, because I knew you'd leave in the end. It was a way to control the hurt. You were guaranteed not to stick around, so I knew in advance what I was getting into. It only came unstuck because I let myself care.'

'You got involved with me because you thought it wouldn't last?' Of all the things he'd thought she might say, that wasn't in the script. She didn't want to care? 'You let yourself care about me despite your best efforts?'

'Was I wrong? First sign of a challenge, and I was left in your dust.' She shrugged as if to tell him she hadn't missed a wink of sleep over the fact. 'And now the challenge has been removed and I'm not Danny's recipient, you've come back for a bit more.' She threw her head back, looked him in the eye and asked, 'How long until you'd be off this time?'

'I already knew I'd messed up and that I wanted to fix things with you before I found out about Danny.'

'It doesn't look that way to me.' Anger—or hurt—was getting the better of her now and two patches of colour had appeared high in her cheeks. With her hair loose like it was, she'd never looked more beautiful and his heart twisted that she seemed hell-bent on shutting him out. 'Why come to Tori's wedding to tell us about this? Why didn't you ring yesterday? Her wedding isn't the right place for her to find out.'

'I rang and told her last night.' Sarah's look of incredulity warned him to tread carefully. 'I asked her not to say anything because I wanted to tell you, and she invited Mum and me to the church today. Mum was thrilled to be able to see her get married, especially as they won't get a chance to meet now until after Tori's honeymoon. And since I wanted to tell you about Danny but she also wanted to talk to you about it before she left, now was the only time. If I didn't get to speak to you, Tori was going to tell you tonight.'

'So you and Tori discussed all this without telling me.'

Both he and Tori had been worried about whether she'd react to being kept in the dark by the sister she so loved, but they'd decided that it was for the greater good. He tried that angle now. 'Tori agreed to give me the chance to set things straight with you—'

Sarah made a sound reflecting her disbelief and searched the crowd, and Ned knew she was looking for her offending sister, not hard to spot in her layered white wedding dress. Luckily for Tori, she was oblivious to the look Sarah sent in her direction, but there was no such luck for Ned. 'She should have known better,' she said as she flicked her glance over him. 'You didn't need to tell me in person and Tori knows that. Even if I believed you thought you wanted to start over, I know better.'

'What does that mean?'

'When you ended it with me, you were back in the pub scene straight away, and you looked fine with

Georgie and goodness knows who else all over you. You looked pretty happy with Georgie just now, too, until you palmed her off onto Scott.'

'You were at the pub that night?' He did a quick mental calculation, thinking back to the first and last time he'd been out since Sarah. 'Of course you were there,' he continued, not needing her to explain because, of course, that's the way his rotten luck was running. The one night he'd been out, the five minutes he'd had a girl all over him, would have been the time Sarah would have seen him. 'Georgie said she was there for a girls' night and here she is again.' It all made sense now. 'She knows Tori. Is that why her friend dragged her away that night, because you were there?'

The patches of colour in her cheeks deepened and spread and she didn't answer. She didn't need to because her anger gave him the brightest glimmer of hope he'd had so far. She was angry because she'd seen him with Georgie that night and she'd been livid to see Georgie on his arm just now. What else could that mean except that she cared about him, despite her claims to not want to? Otherwise, what did it matter how many women he had hanging on him?

'If you know Georgie at all, you'll know that while she's fun, she will also latch onto any guy around. It means nothing. I was that guy for a few minutes that night. You saw her just now run off with Steve.'

'Scott, not Steve,' she corrected, 'and Georgie isn't the point.' For someone who wasn't important she was being mentioned far too often in his opinion, but he let that one slide. 'The point is, you ended things with me as quickly as you could and you didn't miss a beat.'

'But I'm telling you now I know I messed up and I want to start over. Do I mean so little to you you're not willing to try?'

'I can't do that. I'm not like you, Ned.' She ignored his last question and again he took that as a sign she did still care. Not that he had a clue about how to get her to admit that. 'I can't go down that road knowing I'll have to pick up the pieces when you leave again.' Once more, she gestured to someone over his shoulder, looking hassled now. 'I have to run. The photographer is waiting.' She started to walk away then hesitated and placed a hand tentatively on his arm. 'I'm sorry it ended the way it did, Ned. I guess the only good thing to come out of this is Tori and your mum both got what they wanted. They found each other.' For a long moment she held his gaze, her grey eyes luminous with regret. And as she walked away, he could've sworn she whispered, 'I thought we had, too.'

CHAPTER TEN

THERE were more single men at the reception than she'd met all year. Within an hour of the band striking up, they'd each twirled her onto the dance floor with varying degrees of finesse.

Some of them were witty, all of them were pleasant.

None of them were Ned.

And the fact she was still thinking that way made her even madder with herself.

Tori appeared at her side, dragging her away from a stockbroker who, while interesting, wasn't Ned. Not that it's relevant, she scolded herself yet again.

'You're the belle of the ball,' said Tori, ushering her sister into a quiet corner, 'but I'm not sure your heart's in it. I told you at the church Ned could come if you wanted him to. I told him, too, but he said he could only do that if you wanted him here.' She looked around at the many guests. 'So why isn't he here?'

'I have no intention of spending time with a man who is only interested in me when the going is easy and will be off again the moment he gets bored or it's too hard.'

'I thought you two talked today? Didn't he mention

anything other than the mix-up with our files? Didn't he say he wanted to start again?'

'Sure, he said it, but the possibility of Ned wanting to start again for anything longer than twenty-four hours is roughly zero.' She fixed her sister with a firm stare, thoughts dropping into place. She'd been too busy reliving her encounter with Ned to see the gaps in the story but they came to her now. She frowned. 'How did you know he wanted another chance? And why didn't you tell me about the mix-up with Danny? Or that you'd invited Ned and his mother to the wedding?'

'Ned asked me not to.'

'And you listen to Ned rather than doing what's right by me?' She tried to keep the hurt out of her voice but didn't manage it. Not anywhere close. 'Why would you do that? He only came back to me once he knew I wasn't Danny's recipient. That's hardly commitment.'

'I didn't tell you because he wanted to talk to you and when I knew why it was so important to him, I knew it was what was best for you, too, even if you can't see that right now. And as for only wanting you once he knew about Danny, that's not true.'

'It's easy to say that when he already knew about the mix-up.'

'He worked it out before—'

Tori stopped and flushed, which made Sarah immediately suspicious. When did Tori ever feel embarrassed or guilty? They were all wasted emotions according to her. 'How would you know that?'

Her twin was stalling for time, waving to someone across the room. Sarah knew her inside and out and she knew the wave was pretence. 'I can't say,' she replied when she'd finished greeting a non-existent person. 'You'll have to ask Ned.'

Sarah spoke aloud as she worked it out. 'You spoke to him before last night when he rang to tell you about the mix-up. You've spoken to him some other time and haven't told me.'

'I can't say anything.' Tori opened her eyes wide in an appeal for leniency, holding her hands up in mock protection. 'Besides, don't shoot the messenger. What I'm saying is if *he* says he already knew how much you meant to him, you should believe him and not get side-tracked by the mix-up issue.'

'I will find out what you're hiding, Tori.' But she softened her statement with a smile.

'Think about what I've said. And, more importantly, think about what Ned told you earlier. If you can believe he knew what you meant to him before the mix-up was discovered, ask yourself whether it's really not worth the risk in trying again. You're in love with him, Sarah. Isn't it worth taking a risk or two for that?'

Harry arrived beside them then, ready to whisk Tori onto the dance floor.

Watching them as they spun away, watching Harry holding Tori with such gentleness that she might have been made of porcelain, gazing with rapt attention into each other's eyes, all Sarah could feel was very, very lonely.

Lonely and confused.

Ned was a short-term guy, and he'd been off the first chance he'd got. If he came back to her, he'd do it again. Even his friends said that's who he was.

People didn't change. Ned wouldn't change, no

matter what he had Tori believing. Tori was simply being influenced by her own happy ending, willing it to happen for her twin.

Sarah shrugged, trying to stir up the fighting spirit that was at her core, the belief that at least if she hadn't got the happy ending she'd wanted, she'd still achieved one of a different making.

For the first time in her adult life she knew implicitly that she was going to be OK. Somehow the hurt over thinking her flaws had had some part to play in Ned leaving had made her embrace those flaws. She now accepted her scar and the fact she'd had a transplant had not caused Ned to leave. Finding out about Danny had been the catalyst for that. The fact he was a happy-go-lucky bachelor with enough natural charm for a roomful of men made it certain he'd never be back by her side for long.

So she'd been with a man who could have any woman he wanted and still desired her, despite what she'd come to think of as her failings. Because of that, she'd realised none of those things made her less than whole. Nothing could unless she thought about herself that way.

She couldn't believe Ned's claim that he wanted to start over, because starting over wasn't the same as staying the distance.

She should never have let herself get into that situation. She never would again.

Firm resolve was one thing, but it still left a girl lonely on a night like this.

She needed a booster shot of self-belief.

She made her way over to the DJ.

'I'm calling bridesmaid's rights on choosing the next song.' She named a couple of classic break-up songs. 'I'm open to suggestions, as long as it qualifies for women's anthem status.'

As the first song began, couples moved apart to dance as singles, groups of women surged together and a few men slipped away to the sidelines as the lyrics blared out. Sarah stepped into the moving mass of bodies, buoyed by a rush of exhilaration. Ned may have left a gaping hole in heart but for the first time in her life she felt whole.

She was good enough. Just the way she was.

And she deserved to be treated as such.

Sarah clicked the DVD out of its case and slid it into the machine. She needed a dose of chick-flick magic to get her through the day ahead.

She curled up on the couch, pointed the remote at the screen, hit the play button and willed herself to be whisked away into a world where someone else messed up and had their heart broken. After the night she'd had, she was well and truly sick of her own broken heart.

She'd spent the rest of the reception on the dance floor, psyching herself up for a world with no Ned in it. Then she'd spent most of the early hours of the morning tossing and turning on her bed, unable to sleep. She'd managed to enjoy the wedding. But the loneliness had hit her once she'd returned home.

It was all very well singing about self-belief at the top of her lungs on the dance floor, but the morning after was devoid of the same passion. She wanted the man she loved.

Which brought her full circle to the root of the problem. The man she loved was a playboy she would never have.

A charming playboy, but a playboy all the same.

The doorbell chimed and she jumped. Tori and Harry would be on the plane by now, en route to their honeymoon destination, and she wasn't expecting anyone.

She rubbed her head as the sound rang through the house again. She hadn't drunk more than the obligatory glass of champagne for the toasts last night but the lack of sleep had left her feeling less than well this morning.

Sighing, she pushed herself to her feet, and padded down the hallway.

Through the stained-glass window beside the front door she could see what looked suspiciously like a tan fire-retardant jacket with a fluorescent orange armband. Probably her imagination playing tricks, but she checked her reflection in the hall mirror just in case, quickly applying a slash of lip gloss and fluffing her hair up with her fingers.

With her heart racing and hoping for the best even while her common sense hissed *He's a playboy* in her ear, she threw open the door.

And was hit with an intense surge of disappointment.

Her visitor was wearing a fireman's uniform but it wasn't Ned.

'Sarah Richardson?'

She nodded, not even attempting to summon up a smile. What was there to be happy about?

'I have a delivery for you. It's your silent auction prize.'

The letter she'd received had stated she'd won one of the items but hadn't specified which one. She'd bid on several but for the life of her she couldn't think what any of them were. She looked down at his hands but they were empty. No clues there. She was sure she hadn't been so daft as to bid on the Bachelor of the Year. She looked up again. 'What—?' Her question lodged in her throat as she saw, past the young fireman's shoulder, rising above her front fence the extension arm of an aerial appliance.

In the basket, hovering clear above the height of her fence, was Ned.

She glanced back at the young fireman, who was looking suspiciously like the Cheshire cat. 'You won a ride in an appliance.' He held his arm out towards her front gate. 'If you'd like to come this way.'

Sarah followed him out of her house and across the street. The appliance was parked in the church car park opposite her house and several of her neighbours were already milling around. She was vaguely aware of all that, but she only had eyes for Ned. Even when he was four metres above her she could still feel the magnetic pull of attraction.

He was smiling now, his grin wide. Even from this distance she could still see the dark shadow of his dimple in his cheek, could still see his green eyes flashing with mirth.

He raised a loudhailer to his lips. 'Personal delivery for Sarah Richardson.' She thought the loudhailer was a tad unnecessary but it seemed he had a clear idea of how this was going to go. Glad one of us does, was all she could think, scrambling to fill in the blanks. 'A personal ride hosted by yours truly on, in colloquial terms, a fire engine. And, yes…' He raised his helmet to the small cluster of onlookers hanging on his every word. 'The fair lady is allowed to put the siren on, so be ready to cover your ears.'

'I'll take it if you don't want to,' offered three of her neighbours at once when Sarah failed to reply immediately. They were all middle-aged, all women, and all looking very eagerly at Ned as they addressed Sarah. All willing to seize the moment, all willing to have some fun.

Tori's words from last night rang in Sarah's ears. 'You are in love with him, Sarah. Isn't it worth taking a risk or two for that?'

There was a seriously adorable man publicly wooing her. A man she'd sent packing just yesterday. A man who'd come back in style to—to what?

All of a sudden common sense whacked her over the skull and told her if she missed this opportunity, she deserved to never have anything good happen again.

This was her scene and she was going to reclaim it.

'Sorry to disappoint you,' she said to the spectators, while looking at Ned, 'but this package is all mine.' She took one step. Then another and another until she was almost directly under the basket, with Ned smiling enigmatically down at her, looking so very masculine and at home that her heart fluttered just as her twin sister had accused it of doing.

'You heard it here, folks, this ride is all hers, and yours truly is part of the package,' said Ned through the loudhailer, ensuring everyone could hear, before he lowered it to his side and said to her alone, 'Now we just need to work out what that actually means.'

'Can I come up so we can talk in private?'

Ned lazily surveyed the assembled crowd before pinning her with his gaze. 'You have a strange definition of private, but if you're game, so am I.'

She watched as Ned pressed a button and the basket started a slow descent towards her. One of the other firemen hopped out of the truck and led her to a ladder at the rear, indicating she needed to climb it. She gathered the hem of her sundress in her hand, trying to preserve a little of her dignity as she scrambled up the ladder to the roof of the appliance.

Ned was waiting for her.

He swung the gate open and leant forward to help her inside, pulling her in with ease before securing the gate. The basket jerked slightly then with a grinding noise slowly rose above the crowd who were watching them with fascinated anticipation. She watched the ground recede below them and nothing could have prevented the grin she knew was spreading across her face at the feeling that she'd stepped beyond the usual confines of her life.

'There's not a lot of room up here,' she said as she turned and found herself very close indeed to the man who was responsible both for breaking her heart and teaching her she was fine just the way she was. She was still to work out how those two lessons went together, but she knew they did.

'Scared of heights?'

'I've been scared of lots of things—luckily it turns out heights isn't one of them.' She jumped a little as the cage jerked to a halt, and added, 'Even with the turbulence.'

'Tell me what you're scared of.' He'd dropped his

head so his mouth was only an inch from hers, his voice a deep, rich, shivery whisper. 'I'm sure I can help.'

'I'm counting on it.' She took a breath, a deep one, and pitched head first into her speech, encouraged by the fact he was there. What woman wouldn't take that as a very healthy sign? 'First, I have some questions.'

'Shoot.'

'Why does Tori believe you when you say you want to start again?'

'I knew this would come out sooner or later.' He threw his hands up to indicate he'd been caught out but he didn't look remotely worried by the prospect. 'Tori's my counsellor.'

'Your what?'

'Counsellor, you know, someone who helps you work through—'

She poked him in the ribs. 'I know what a counsellor is. How come you needed one and how on earth did it end up being Tori?'

'I needed to talk things over with someone, because the one thing I knew was that I was miserable after we stopped seeing each other and I couldn't see how that fitted together with you being Danny's heart recipient. And it was Tori I saw for the simple reason I was loitering outside the foundation building, contemplating my messed-up head, when she came by. She knew a likely customer when she saw one. I was crying out to be helped.'

'You were miserable without me?'

She looked and sounded like she was really hearing him, unlike yesterday. What had happened to change her attitude towards him? He didn't know, but the thought spurred him on. 'Utterly useless. I even had physical symptoms that had me wondering about angina.'

'Really? And you really had counselling with Tori?'

He traced his finger in a cross over his heart. 'Truly. On all counts. I was a model client. A talented one, too, because by the end of the session we had it all worked out. I've been a dolt and whether or not every single organ in your body was donated by Danny is irrelevant to how I feel about you.' He tilted his head. 'And I have given Tori my full permission to answer any question you have so you can verify for yourself that I knew what you meant to me before I knew about the mix-up at the foundation.'

'But why didn't you tell me this yesterday?'

'I had about three minutes. I gave it my best shot but I think there was quite a lot I managed not to say. Hence today. I figured I'd double my chances of a good hearing if I turned up in a show-stopper.'

'I admit it got your foot in the door. But what else didn't you tell me?'

'It took about ten minutes of talking things through with Tori to work out why I was having trouble breathing. That's how I reacted to my dad's and Danny's deaths. I just stopped breathing properly. Mum tried all sorts of things with me but the only thing that worked was swimming. I became obsessed with it. When I stopped seeing you my chest constriction started again and I only saw that link with Tori's help. So then I knew what I had to do. I had to win you back.

'I hadn't planned on talking to you until after the wedding. I knew from Tori you were flat out and I didn't want to distract you from enjoying the day. But that all changed when Mum and I found out Danny was Tori's donor. Tori had already been sent a letter saying her donor family agreed to contact and Mum really wanted her to know before the wedding. Mum thought it would give them both the answers they were after. But that meant you needed to know too and that's the reason I came. It wasn't the timing I would've chosen, but it had to be that way.'

'It wasn't perfect, I admit.' She smiled. 'You would have done better if you hadn't had Georgie draped all over you.'

He grimaced. 'Worst run of luck in the world. I went away racking my brain about what to do next as you didn't believe me. I got so desperate I even asked Phoebe and Max's opinion when I got home after the wedding. Actually, I didn't ask for Max's but he offered it anyway. But Phoebe…' He stroked his chin, nodding. 'Now, Phoebe had some good advice. When I was bemoaning the fact you hadn't believed me when I'd said what you meant to me, she asked me if I'd actually told you what you meant to me.'

'And had you?'

'No. For all my practice, it turns out I neglected to tell you I want to start over because I love you.' Sarah gasped and clutched at the bar behind her. He knew an opportunity when he saw one, so he reached out and pulled her into his arms. He pretended it was so she didn't tumble out of the basket but there was no risk of that. He needed her in his arms when he said what he was about to say. 'I'm in love with you. I want us to have it all.' A shadow of doubt chased away the joy that had blossomed on her face a moment before. 'What is it?'

'What happens later?'

He kissed her nose. 'Meeting you has made me see my life was filled with meaningless chatter, white noise so I didn't have to risk feeling, getting close to someone. If I did that, I'd risk getting hurt again so I created a life where I had no chance of meeting someone I could love. I surrounded myself with mates at work and women who only saw the uniform. And then you came along...' he tugged a lock of her hair '...cleverly disguised as a colleague and sneaked in when my guard was down. I never had a chance. You were what I'd needed all along, precisely why I worked so hard to sabotage it. To make absolutely sure you understand me, I'll say it again.' He took her hand and raised it to his lips, continuing to hold it afterwards. 'I love you. I love everything about you. I love it that you have a killer career, I love it that you can stand on your own two feet, take on whatever comes your way and hit it for six. And I love it that, despite all that, when I kiss you, you're a woman through and through. A soft, yielding, meltingly delicious woman.'

She sighed, the noise escaping from her throat on a tiny kitten-like note.

'I love it that you make me laugh, you challenge me, and we can talk, really talk. I love it that my friends like you and you like them. And, somewhat strangely, I love it that my mum thinks you're adorable and she hasn't even met you properly yet.' He tugged on her hand and she didn't resist, coming into his embrace and nestling against him as if there'd never been any distance between them. 'I love it that when we make love, there is no room in my head for anything beyond being with you, in your arms, with you in mine.'

'That's a whole lot of love.'

'Correction,' he said as he tilted her chin up with his left hand, 'you are a whole lot to love.'

'I am?'

'You are, but don't interrupt a man on a roll.' He cleared his throat and continued. 'You are also the only woman who has ever fascinated me. Fascinated and impressed me, every inch of you. You are perfection all bundled up in a delectable package. And I am here, not just now but for ever if you want me, ready and willing to adore you and encourage you and support you in everything you are and everything you want to be. I admit I messed up something infinitely simple, but I'm a man. And if I wasn't sure, I wouldn't do what I am about to do now in such a public fashion.'

He took a step backwards—not much more was possible in the confines of the cage—and raised the loud-hailer again, his eyes sliding to hers, fixed in amused disbelief on his. 'It's down to my secret past in the Boy Scouts. I hate being caught unprepared so, unlike yesterday, I came ready to combat your lack of auditory ability.'

He wouldn't.

Would he?

He fixed her with a long look that had her toes curling in delicious anticipation. 'Think we need it?'

'Personally, I think I can hear you without it, but I'd hate to be accused of ruining a carefully crafted moment.' She nodded her head to indicate the spectators below. 'There are a lot of people down there waiting to be impressed.'

'There is that. Then again, my bag of tricks is totally empty after this. It seems a shame to start on such a high point and have it all go downhill from here.'

'I'm listening now but...' she gripped the loudhailer around the base and lifted it further so it was in front of his lips '...just to make sure I hear you...'

Ned's smile started in his eyes and she could feel it, too, in the warmth of his touch as he closed his hand over hers, hitting the on button as he did so. 'For those of you still down there, I have just told this magnificent woman here with me that I love her.' He kept his eyes focused on her as hoots and hollers floated up to them from below, carrying her spirits high into the air with them. 'Today also marks the one and only time I will ever ask the woman I love to marry me.' He was watching her closely. She knew he was waiting for her reaction, but other than a great big goofy smile she wasn't yet capable of anything more. 'Ladies and gentleman, I'll get back to you with her response, but the early word is she looks pleased.'

He took her hand, gently rubbing her ring finger as he flicked the loudhailer off, speaking just to her. 'I love you. If you want me, I am yours, and if for ever isn't too short-term a commitment for you, that's where I'm suggesting we start. I don't think I can take another night without knowing you are mine, not to sound too proprietorial, but last night almost killed me, thinking of you being surrounded by all those other men at the wedding. You're not meant to be with other men. You're meant to be with me.' The note of certainty in his voice sent rivers of treacled warmth down her spine.

'I am meant to be with you,' she replied.

'See how easy it is when you listen to me?'

From down below, someone yelled up, 'What's the answer?'

'Seems we still have spectators. Would you like to put them out of their misery or shall I?'

She retrieved the loudhailer, hit the on button and raised it to her lips. 'The answer is yes!' she announced, before letting the equipment slide to her side on the floor of the basket as the horn on the fire engine blared in response to her announcement and her neighbours called out their approval. 'The next part of my response is not for sharing,' she said as she stood on tiptoe and found Ned's mouth with hers, the world about them receding as they shared a kiss that was full of promises for the future, their future.

Coming up for air, Ned ran his hands down Sarah's arms, taking her hands in his again. 'I liked the second part of your answer. A lot.'

She laughed and swatted him on the arm for his over-playing of the lover's role. 'I have to tell you this. I'm sorry I was so dense yesterday. If I'd listened then, our for ever would've started last night.'

He slid a hand up her back, making every nerve-ending in her body light up with that one smooth movement. 'I'm sure you'll make it up to me.'

'We can start now.' She laughed as he dodged her attempt to find his lips again, impatient to give in to her electric reaction to him.

'You haven't told me what made you start listening. Me, the truck or the uniform?'

She tugged at the heavy overcoat zipped up, preventing any chance of splaying her hands over his chest, bare or otherwise. 'I hate to tell you that, notwithstanding your dramatic and much-appreciated fulfilment of the hero role just now, I'd already worked out I'd been an idiot. I realised that to let you go because I was afraid of losing you made precisely no sense at all.' She slid her fingers into the top opening of his thick coat and tugged impatiently. 'Did I mention I'm hungry to be kissed again?'

'Don't be so impatient. Me or the truck? Or the uniform?'

'All right, it's you. With or without the uniform. But as for the truck…'

'Mmm-hmm?'

'That was a definite plus.' It seemed the most natural thing in the world. She could scarcely believe she hadn't known all along it would turn out this way. 'But I would like to know whether I'm going to wake up every Sunday to find a fire truck parked in our driveway or was this a one-off?'

'It qualifies as a slight one-off bending of the regulations. Training isn't scheduled on Sundays. Since I got the silent auction winner's list on Friday, I deemed today "fulfil silent auction bid day". You were top of the list. Or at least you were when I read it back to front.'

He kissed her on the tip of her nose.

'There's one more thing.'

'I'm not sure I knew you talked this much, but go on.' He pulled on her hair and she wrinkled her nose at him in silent retort.

'You promise to only wear your uniform out to the pub when I'm with you.'

'Ah, so it is a turn-on.' He edged closer, breathing in her scent, feeling the tightness in his body display his need for her. 'It wasn't me and it wasn't the truck.'

'Yup, it's all about the uniform.'

'Then I solemnly swear…' he drew a line across the left of his chest '…to do as you ask.'

She let go of his hands and wrapped her arms around him. 'Thanks. Now I've finished talking and I need to be kissed again.'

'It would be my pleasure.' He pulled her into his embrace, hugging her close, before bending his head to claim her mouth with his.

Sarah was vaguely aware of the cage jarring into motion as it started to descend but after that nothing had a chance to penetrate her consciousness, which was full to bursting with the rainbow-coloured sensations being thoroughly kissed by Ned evoked. She had a vague awareness of cheers and applause and a loud blare of a siren, all as if in the far-off distance, but nothing could touch the bubble of happiness enveloping her.

How could anything be a match for the discovery they'd made, the discovery that her destined place in the world was here, in Ned's arms, for ever?

She wrapped her fingers around his neck, breathed in deeply to fill her head with the scent of him, and drifted away on a cloud of magical sensations as he kissed her as though it was the last kiss on earth.

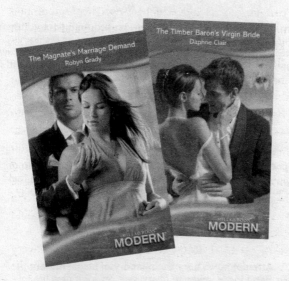

THE ROYAL HOUSE OF KAREDES

Two crowns, two islands, one legacy

Volume One
**BILLIONAIRE PRINCE,
PREGNANT MISTRESS**
by Sandra Marton

Wanted for her body – and her baby!

Aspiring New York jewellery designer Maria Santo has come to Aristo to win a royal commission.

Cold, calculating and ruthless, Prince Xander Karedes beds Maria, thinking she's only sleeping with him to save her business.

So when Xander discovers Maria's pregnant, he assumes it's on purpose. What will it take for this billionaire prince to realise he's falling in love with his pregnant mistress…?

Available 17th April 2009

www.millsandboon.co.uk

IN HIS POWER...
AND IN HIS BED?

Featuring these three passionate stories:

Desert Prince, Blackmailed Bride
by Kim Lawrence

The Marcolini Blackmail Marriage
by Melanie Milburne

Dante's Blackmailed Bride by Day Leclaire

Available 17th April 2009

www.millsandboon.co.uk

M&B

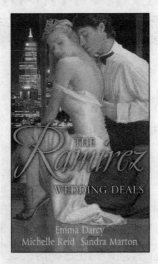
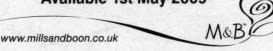

2 FREE

BOOKS AND A SURPRISE GIFT!

We would like to take this opportunity to thank you for reading this Mills & Boon® book by offering you the chance to take TWO more specially selected titles from the Medical™ series absolutely FREE! We're also making this offer to introduce you to the benefits of the Mills & Boon® Book Club™—

- ★ **FREE home delivery**
- ★ **FREE gifts and competitions**
- ★ **FREE monthly Newsletter**
- ★ **Exclusive Mills & Boon Book Club offers**
- ★ **Books available before they're in the shops**

Accepting these FREE books and gift places you under no obligation to buy, you may cancel at any time, even after receiving your free shipment. Simply complete your details below and return the entire page to the address below. You don't even need a stamp!

YES! Please send me 2 free Medical books and a surprise gift. I understand that unless you hear from me, I will receive 4 superb new titles every month for just £2.99 each, postage and packing free. I am under no obligation to purchase any books and may cancel my subscription at any time. The free books and gift will be mine to keep in any case.

M9ZED

Ms/Mrs/Miss/Mr ....Initials ....

BLOCK CAPITALS PLEASE

Surname ....

Address ....

....

....Postcode...............................

Send this whole page to:
UK: FREEPOST CN81, Croydon, CR9 3WZ

Offer valid in UK only and is not available to current Mills & Boon Book Club subscribers to this series. Overseas and Eire please write for details and readers in Southern Africa write to Box 3010, Pinegowie, 2123 RSA. We reserve the right to refuse an application and applicants must be aged 18 years or over. Only one application per household. Terms and prices subject to change without notice. Offer expires 30th June 2009. As a result of this application, you may receive offers from Harlequin Mills & Boon and other carefully selected companies. If you would prefer not to share in this opportunity please write to The Data Manager, PO Box 676, Richmond, TW9 1WU.

Mills & Boon® is a registered trademark owned by Harlequin Mills & Boon Limited.
Medical™ is being used as a trademark. The Mills & Boon® Book Club™ is being used as a trademark.